March in

Michael Carroll of Bantry w... family whose ancestors were ...ged in piracy during the seventeenth century, while others signed the American Declaration of Independence. During the 1950s and 1960s he studied and travelled widely and then became involved in both the Whiddy Oil Terminal and the shipping business. After retiring in the late 1980s he began his research and writing. Over the next ten years he published *The Second Spanish Armada*, *Where the Deer Ran Wild*, *A Bay of Destiny*, *Wolfe Tone and the French Invasion*, *The Castles and Fortified Houses of West Cork*, plus many leaflets on archaeology and local tourist guides.

Amongst his forthcoming publications, due next year, are *Night Riders* and *Atlantic Tsunami*.

Michael Carroll lives in Bantry and runs the Bantry Bookstore.

This book is dedicated to the memory of all the O'Sullivan Bere clan, their allies both Irish and Spanish, especially all those who died during the epic march to Leitrim and those who sought refuge with the O'Carrolls

ACKNOWLEDGEMENTS

With the four hundred anniversary of the Sack of Dunboy Castle and the subsequent epic march of O'Sullivan Bere from Glengarriff to Leitrim being commemorated from next year many people have asked me to write a detailed history of Donal Cam O'Sullivan Bere.

After much deliberation I decided to write a historical novel based on intensive research and as close to actual fact as possible.

I thank Rhiannon Shelley for correcting and editing my original script, Brendan for typesetting the manuscript, my colleagues in the book trade who have supplied me with rare material of the period, my mother and son who have been patient during the long days and nights, and Jeremy Irons who urged me on to finish this important episode of Irish history.

MARCH INTO OBLIVION

Michael J Carroll

Bantry Studio Publications

Text © 2001 Michael J Carroll

Published by Bantry Studio Publications, Bantry, Co. Cork, Ireland

First published in 2001

First issued as a Bantry Studio Publication paperback 2001

All rights reserved. No part of this publication may be reproduced, stored in a retrieval system or transmitted in any form or by any means, electronic, mechanical, photocopying, recording or otherwise, without prior permission of Bantry Studio Publications.

This book is sold subject to the conditions that it shall not, by way of trade or otherwise, be lent, re-sold, hired out or otherwise circulated without the publisher's prior consent in any form of binding or cover other than that in which it is published and without a similar condition including this condition being imposed on a subsequent purchase.

ISBN: 0 9519415 4 2

Cover illustration, maps and b/w illustrations by
Alan Langford, Calmane, Southampton, England
Printed in Ireland by Techman (Ireland) Ltd.

Contents

Maps	vi–x
Main Characters	xi–xiv
Introduction	1
Chapter One: After the Battle	8
Chapter Two: The Journey Westward	19
Chapter Three: Dunboy Castle	30
Chapter Four: False Rumours	39
Chapter Five: Carew's Army on the Move	46
Chapter Six: Surprise Attack	54
Chapter Seven: The Fall of Dunboy	63
Chapter Eight: Another Spanish Ship	72
Chapter Nine: The Final Struggle	80
Chapter Ten: Abandoning Camp	86
Chapter Eleven: The First Encounter	94
Chapter Twelve: Running Battle	101
Chapter Thirteen: Desperation	110
Chapter Fourteen: The Crossing	117
Chapter Fifteen: Further Danger	126
Chapter Sixteen: Hunted	132
Chapter Seventeen: Regeneration and Rejection	139
Chapter Eighteen: The Voyage	147
Chapter Nineteen: Exile	155
Chapter Twenty: Spain	163
Poem: Bantry Bay	172

Map of O'Sullivan territory

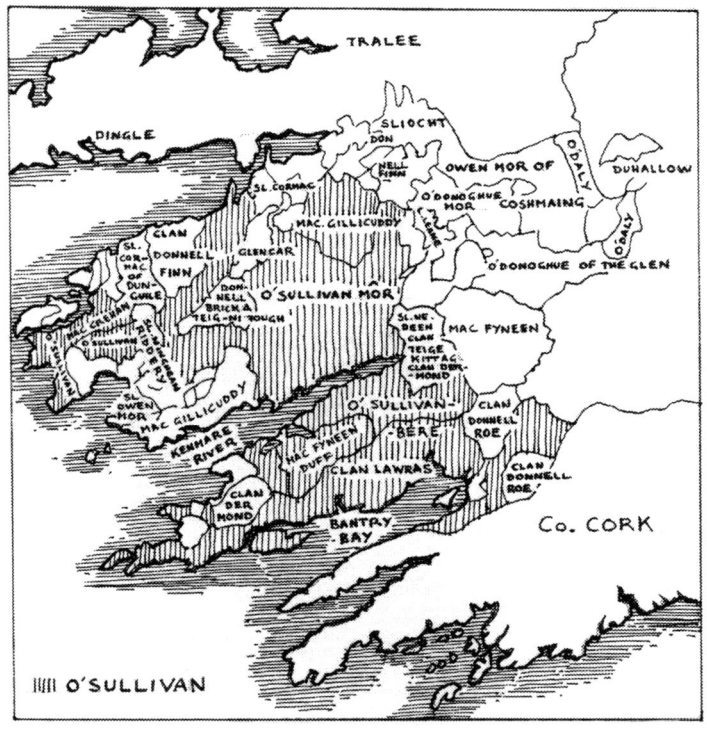

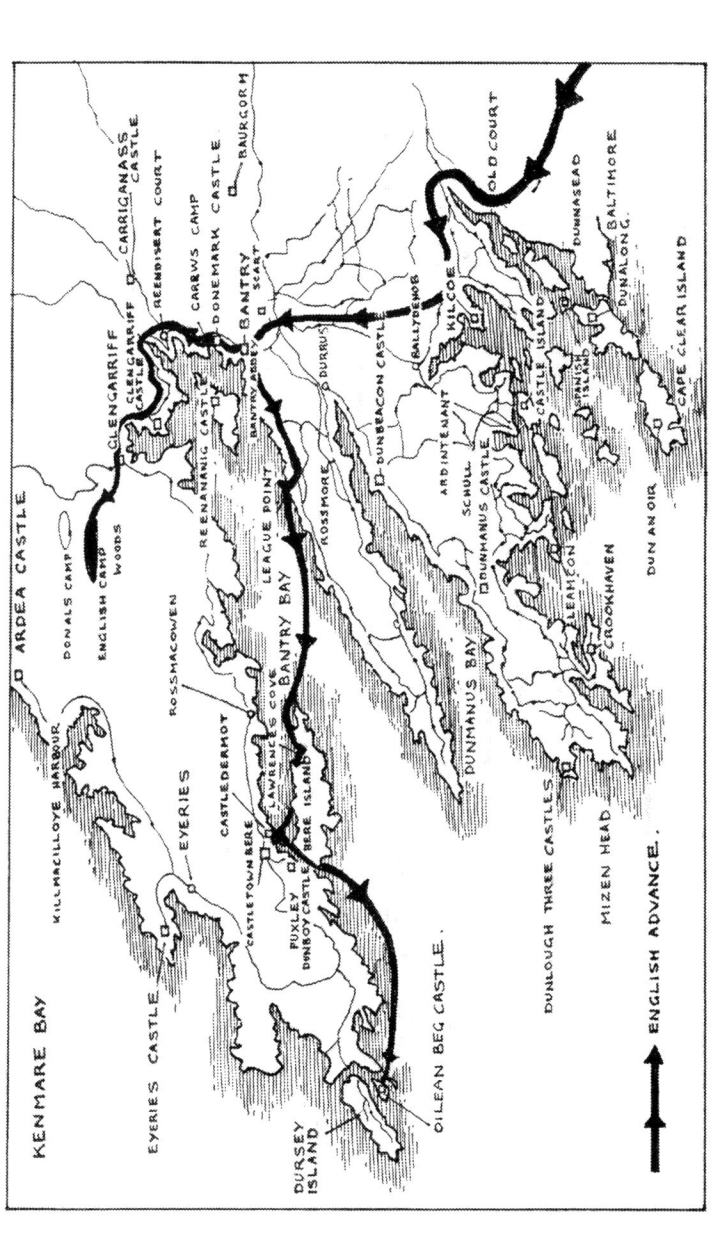
CAREW'S ARMY MOVEMENTS

FIRST PART OF MARCH

SECOND PART OF MARCH

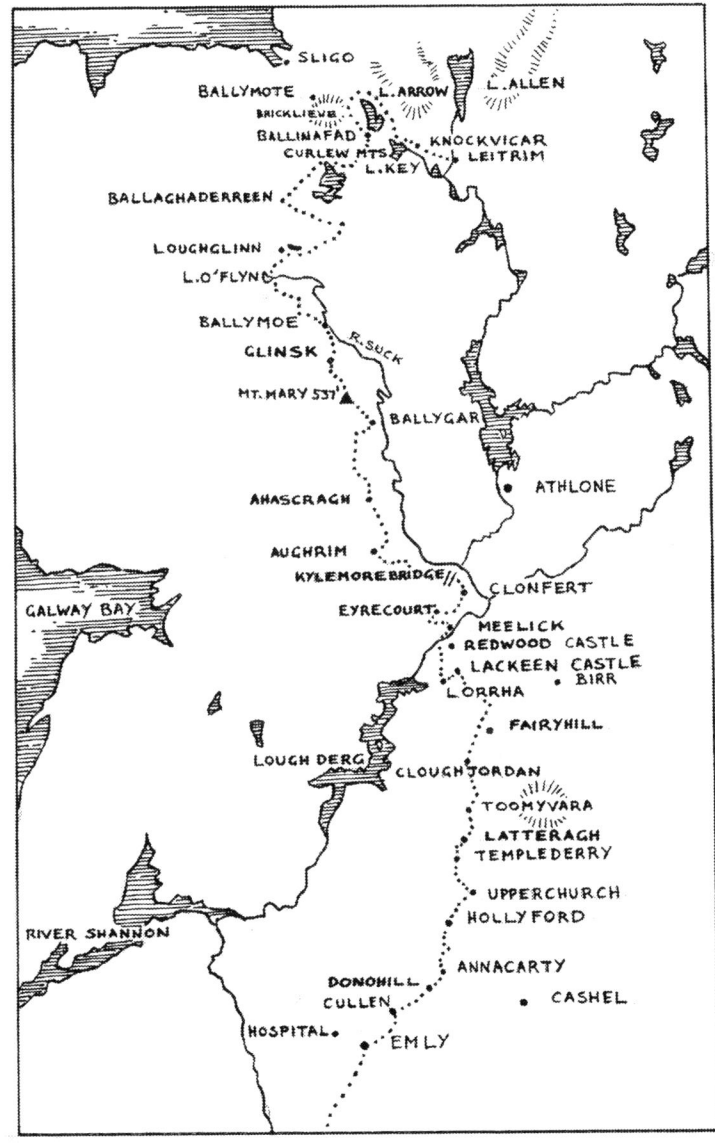

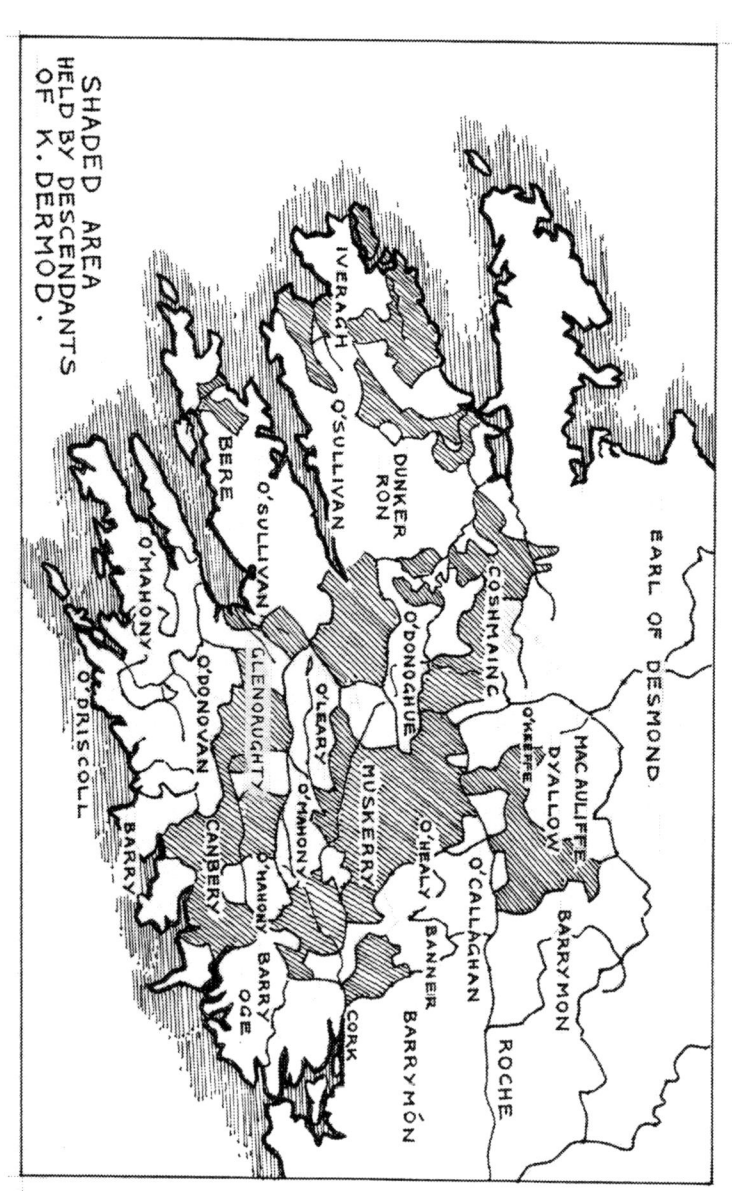

MAIN CHARACTERS (IRISH SIDE)

Donal Cam (limp) O'Sullivan, Prince of Bere, son of Dermod O'Sullivan, (1560–1618)

Dermot O'Sullivan (Dermot Dursey), elderly uncle of Donal who accompanied him on the march to Leitrim.

Hugh O'Neill, Earl of Tyrone (1540–1616), fought at Kinsale. Submitted to Lord Mountjoy in April 1603. Sailed into exile with Rory O'Donnell from Lough Swilly. Died in Rome.

Hugh Roe O'Donnell (1571–1602), fought at Kinsale. Younger than Donal and Hugh. Even though he was a brilliant tactician and general he was tempestuous and prone to make sudden decisions without weighing up the consequences. His impetuous action at Kinsale was the main cause of the Irish defeat. He sailed from Castlehaven to seek further help from Spain but died suddenly there. It is reputed that he was poisoned by an English spy.

Rory O'Donnell (1575–1607) brother to Hugh Roe O'Donnell. Fought at Kinsale and led his brother's army back north and became chieftain on Rory's death in Spain. Like O'Neill he surrendered to Mountjoy. Departed into exile with O'Neill and also died in Rome.

Richard Tyrell was one of O'Neill's mercenary leaders with his own army of gallowglasses and kerns. He was an able tactician and feared by the English with his guerrilla warfare. He was pardoned by King James on or about the time that Donal Cam sailed for Spain.

William Burke was also one of O'Neill's mercenary leaders like Tyrell with his own army of gallowglasses and kerns. He accompanied Donal Cam in his march to Leitrim and was later pardoned with Tyrell.

Philip O'Sullivan, Táiniste of the O'Sullivans, uncle of Donal Cam, who lived at Ardea Castle on Kenmare Bay.

Philip O'Sullivan (1590–?), youngest son of Dermod Dursey and first cousin of Donal Cam. Sent to Spain in 1602. Studied at the Irish College at Salamanca. Became a soldier and then served in the Spanish navy. He was a prolific writer and amongst his works in Latin was the Historiae Catholicae Compendium which gave some details of the March to Leitrim which were dictated to him by his father before he died.

The O'Driscolls—Donal, Dermod, Cornelius, Teige and Darby—who were in occupation of Castlehaven and Baltimore castles.

MAIN CHARACTERS (ENGLISH SIDE)

Sir George Carew, Lord President of Munster(1555–1629). Shrewd military man well used to psychological warfare and who relied on a network of spies. He suffered from ill- health yet despite this he successfully planned out every action in detail.

Lord Mountjoy, Lord Deputy of Ireland. He was a ruthless man and his motto was to kill and lay waste the country to gain the upper hand over the Irish.

Sir Charles Wilmot (1570–1644). He was Carew's right hand man. In 1603 after the destruction of Dunboy castle and the flight of the O'Sullivans he laid waste Beara, but suffered severe losses due to the adverse weather conditions. He later became President of Connaught and Viscount of Athlone.

Sir Owen O'Sullivan of Carriganass - died 1594 - who claimed the chieftainship after Donal Cam's father's death and with whom he contested the leadership.

Owen O'Sullivan Jr. who died in the same year as Donal Cam.

He, like his father, sided with the English. Became Lord of Bantry in 1594 and Lord of Bantry and Beara from 1603 to 1618 during Donal Cam's absence/exile.

Captain Harveys - two brothers - in the service of Carew - and who participated in the conquest of West Cork.

Captain Flower, also in the service of Carew who was third in command and who participated in the siege of Dunboy.

The Earl of Thomond - Donough O'Brien, chieftain - who was the main ally of the English in Munster and who supplied them with most of the Anglo Irish forces who took part in the siege of Dunboy.

MacCarthy Reagh, who at that time sided with the English and who supplied them with over four hundred men.

Charles Mac Carthy, Chief of Muskerry, who also sided with the English but under duress.

Following the defeat at Kinsale the following was the situation in Munster and West Cork.

THE IRISH SIDE

The following were the main chieftains who assisted Donal Cam O'Sullivan after the Battle of Kinsale:

Daniel MacCarthy, Chief of Clancarthy.
Daniel, son of O'Sullivan Mór of Desmond.
Cornelius and Dermot, sons of O'Driscoll Mór of Baltimore.
Dermot, Donogh and Florence of the MacCarthy Reaghs.
The MacSweeneys of West Cork and Kerry.
The O'Mahonys of Carbery.
The O'Donoghues of the Glen (Kerry).

The O'Donovan's of Leap.
O'Connor Kerry of Desmond.
Knight of Glen.
John Fitzpatrick brother of the Earl of Desmond.
Whole army approximately 2,500 men.

On the English side were the following:
Carew's Irish allies from north Munster.
The Irish Auxiliaries.
Duke of Ormond's forces.
MacCarty Reagh.
Barry More, Viscount Buttevant.
O'Donovan of Castledonovan.
The White Knight. Dermot O'Sullivan, brother of O'Sullivan Mór.
Whole army approximately 4,000 men + 500 English soldiers.

Introduction

At the end of the twelfth century Corca Laidhe, the area we know today as West Cork, was in a state of turmoil. Still a land of impenetrable forests and bogs, wild rivers and towering mountains, it was divided along territorial lines that every tribe defended with ferocious determination. Into this society, which was nonetheless highly stratified and organised under ancient Brehon law, the Norman invaders had exploded in 1169. They brought with them an alien system, which would later be known as feudalism, as well as their expertise in the military and construction fields. Soon they were throwing their sturdy castles up all along the coastline, and further emasculating the indigenous clans by laying claim to any adjoining land.

The situation was exacerbated when the Normans began to force the tribes of north Munster out of their hereditary territories, bringing about a forced migration into West Cork. The area was quickly becoming overcrowded, as family after family flocked into what was seen as a place of refuge, a stronghold of Irish resistance.

Amongst those tribes moving southwards was the O'Sullivan clan, whose lands covered the area around modern day Cahir in South Tipperary, with a central seat located around the great mound overlooking the Suir river at Knockgraffon. In the face of pressure from three Norman families—the Butlers to the north, O'Briens to the west and Fitzgeralds to the south, they gathered up their possessions and made their way through the hostile countryside. They settled in south Kerry, around Bantry and the Beara peninsula, where they leased lands from the powerful McCarthy clan. The MacCarthys had themselves migrated southwards, some forty years earlier, when they had established their hold on the greater part of Cork and Kerry. As their subjects, the O'Sullivans were obliged to render dues, either in money or in kind, to feed their mercenaries, supply men in times of battle and entertain the MacCarthys whenever they visited. Although they were neither particularly strong nor wealthy the O'Sullivans, in turn, were able to subject the smaller local tribes to their rule.

Almost upon arrival, the O'Sullivans divided into two distinct family branches, the O'Sullivan Mór and the O'Sullivan Bere. The former gained control of Kerry, except for the area around, and north of Killarney, and part of the western coastal extremities; the latter acquired the Beare peninsula and the Bantry area extending west to Gearhies. The clan spent the following three hundred years or so consolidating their grasp of the territories, building several castles and engaging in an increasingly lucrative sea trade along the southwest coast. They waged war on several neighbours including the O'Mahonys, O'Donoghues, O'Donovans and even on some subsepts of the MacCarthys.

Everything changed with the death of the reigning chieftain, Dermod O'Sullivan of the Powder, who gained his epithet after blowing himself up, and of his brother Amlavus, who was murdered by a relative. Although they were still in a relatively strong position, a certain rot had set in when the O'Sullivan clan was first divided, and the process gained pace now with further divisions. Already a subsept called the Clan-Lawras were in possession of a sizeable tract of land around Adrigole, and other subsepts were now slicing up the territory west of modern day Castletownbere.

In 1563 Dermod's son Donnell was killed by another O'Sullivan, MacGillicuddy of Kerry. According to the laws of Brehon, there should have been a meeting of all the O'Sullivans to decide who would inherit his title, but Donnell's brother Owen chose to ignore the convention. With no regard to the position of his other brothers and their sons, he simply declared himself chieftain and appointed his younger brother Philip as Tánaiste.

An uneasy peace prevailed amongst the rival O'Sullivan factions during the following years, until Donnell's son Donal Cam came of age. Little is known of Donal's early life, except that as an infant he probably resided with his mother at Kilcathrine near Eyeries. Like his father he was then sent to a bardic school near Waterford; boys were usually dispatched at the age of seven or eight, returning only as they approached manhood. With his uncle Owen in residence at Dunboy Castle, Donal went to live with his maternal grandmother at Rossmacowen near Adrigole. The seat of the family, which would have been on the Clan-Lawras side, was probably situated at the Bank where Fontane later built a substantial house using stone from a ruin.

Any references to Donal during his time at Rossmacowen depict a slovenly young man, spending his days stretched out by the fire, carousing with his friends or hunting the wild Beara mountainsides. He was certainly not without courage, as he demonstrated on one occasion when the MacCarthys stopped by to collect cattle in lieu of unpaid dues. Woken from a slumber by his grandmother, Donal jumped to his feet and rushed out to confront his overlord with a sword. After a heated argument he chopped off the chieftain's hand while he was still on horseback, pulled him to the ground and drove the sword into his heart. As his men fled, Donal recalled MacCarthy's oath that he would never rest in his grave until he had ridden as far as far as Dursey to claim what he was due. Taking up the severed hand, he carried it to the most westerly point on the mainland and left it on the rocks, and so fulfilled the chieftain's oath. Afterwards, locals talked of seeing a hand crawling along the rocks, presumably in search of a body.

Aware that the MacCarthys would have revenge in mind, Donal Cam took refuge with his uncle Dermod of Dursey Castle on Oilean Beag. He began to consider his future. Probably in an effort to strengthen his position, at around this time he married a daughter of Donnell O'Brien of Thomond, possibly named Ellen. There is some uncertainty regarding this union, how long his wife lived or the number of children she bore, as some years later his wife is referred to as a daughter of Owen O'Sullivan of Desmond (in Kerry), also Ellen. Considering that the historian Philip O'Sullivan estimates that Donal's uncle Dermod had eighteen children, and was himself an illegitimate child, anything was possible.

With his maturity and bravery thus established, Donal Cam issued his claim as rightful heir to the O'Sullivan Bere chieftainship. His rival and uncle Owen had by this time declared for the English Crown, following the example of his overlord Donnell MacCarthy Mór, and been titled Lord of Beara and Bantry. Donal's claim was supported by his uncle Dermod. Another uncle, Philip of Ardea, also lent quiet assistance, whilst giving the appearance of neutrality. An application was made to the MacCarthy overlords, quoting the Brehon laws regarding succession, but because of their alliance with Owen they declined to enter into the dispute. Sir Owen, however, had fallen out of favour with the English following his involvement in the Desmond rebellion, and so with no possible alternative Donal referred the matter to the Crown.

Over the following years recriminations were made on both sides. Owen had the advantage of being in possession of the title and the lands, but Donal had received an excellent education, and was able to argue his case in language that the English court could understand. He was, meanwhile, tightening his hold on Beara, even venturing east to Bantry with a small force. When he saw an English army occupying the Franciscan abbey there, which had been built by his great grandfather, he was moved to attack regardless of his inferior manpower. The English force of roughly two hundred and fifty men, under Captain Zouch, was taken by surprise and fled back to Cork, leaving about fifty dead. No replacements were sent, and Donal was fired up by his success. He continued to make his presence felt in the Bantry area, using Reenavanny Castle on Whiddy Island as a base. Sir Owen, who was already in the process of bringing English settlers on to the island, was not pleased.

Finally, in around 1594, the matter was resolved. Donal Cam was granted the area west of Adrigole, including its castles, sea trade and so on. Evicted from Dunboy Sir Owen took himself to Carriganass Castle, having received all the lands east of Adrigole, which incorporated Bantry. Thus the O'Sullivan Bere clan was further divided, its internal rifts deepened.

Some two years after the ruling Sir Owen died and was succeeded by his eldest son. Owen Junior achieved a fine match in the form of the daughter of Cormac MacCarthy of Muskerry, who would probably have brought with her a substantial dowry, of which he was very much in need. The enmity between the two branches of the family gradually faded following the death of Sir Owen Senior, until it became customary for Donal to pay regular visits to his cousin at Carriganass.

The story of a relationship between Donal Cam, and Owen's wife, who rather confusingly seems also to have been called Ellen, is open to question. The history books make no mention of such a tryst, but local tradition tells of a burning romance and the birth of a son to the adulterers. By this time, Donal's legitimate children would have been reaching young adulthood. There seem to have been two daughters, and an eldest son Dermod; some historians make no reference to another two sons, said to have been with Donal at the Battle of Kinsale and afterwards sailed to Spain with Donnell O'Driscoll. They may simply have been lost in the pages of time.

The political climate changed with the arrival of Don Zubiaur, as part of the Spanish invasion force, at Castlehaven in 1601. Caught out by the rapid response of English warships, the small force was in dire straits until Donal declared for the Spanish King. He force marched his army of over six hundred men from Dunboy to Castlehaven, making the journey in under twenty-four hours.

Aided by the O'Driscolls as well as the Spaniards, Donal was victorious, and drove the English back to their ships. The Spanish cannons were now mounted on the shore, and the enemy's warships came under a heavy bombardment before they managed to leave the harbour, while Donal Cam was hailed as a hero.

Meanwhile, Hugh O'Neill (the Earl of Tyrone), and 'Red Hugh O'Donnell were rushing southwards to Kinsale, where Don Juan de Aquila's occupying force was under attack from the English and their Irish allies. Upon their arrival, Donal Cam and his men joined what was by now a mighty army of some twenty thousand men, and surrounded the English, resulting in a siege situation. As the weeks and then months passed, disease, starvation and desertion took such a toll that the English were on the verge of suing for peace. Then, against the better judgment of the other chieftains, O'Donnell insisted that they should mount an outright attack, and what happened next is a familiar feature of Irish history. The warriors lost their way in the darkness, gale force winds and heavy rains, and their plans were betrayed; when they reached the enemy camp, the English force was waiting. What ensued on that Christmas Eve of 1601 was a rout, which left over three thousand Irishmen dead or injured.

O'Neill decided to retreat to his home territory, while O'Donnell left his brother to take his men back north and departed for Spain. Donal Cam O'Sullivan was left in charge of the remaining Munster forces and marched them west to Dunboy Castle, knowing that Sir George Carew's army would not be far behind. It soon became the only castle remaining under Irish control.

After months of skirmishing, which prevented Carew's assault on Dunboy, ships were brought in from Cork to transport the English forces to Bere Island by sea and catch Donal unawares. Having forced an advance on the mainland and fortified their position, the English army launched their attack.

Expected Spanish reinforcements never arrived, and the heroic defensive effort of the small Irish force was in vain. Dunboy fell on the eighteenth of June 1602, and the Irish cause was lost. After another six months of fighting, Donal gathered up his depleted force, and began the epic march to O'Rourke's country, in Leitrim. Over a thousand men, women and children set off from Beara, but only thirty-two men and one woman arrived. Donal's plan was to convince the northern chieftains to continue the fight, but he was too late; O'Neill had already sued for peace.

Even with the death of Queen Elizabeth and succession of the Catholic James, Donal Cam was unable to regain title to his lands. With no other option he sailed for Spain, with what remained of his family and friends. The Spanish King honoured him, and he lived on in that country on a sizeable pension until 1619, when he intervened in a family dispute. He was stabbed to death, and only two years later his son Dermod followed him to the grave. The power of the O'Sullivan Beres, who had ruled over western Beara for more than four hundred years, was at an end. What follows is an account, which aims to be as historically accurate as possible, of the life of Donal Cam O'Sullivan from the defeat at Kinsale to his sad end in Spain.

Chapter One

After the Battle

Donal Cam sat alone by the smouldering fire, his head buried in his hands. He was bewildered and in shock, frozen and soaked to the skin. Gone was the sound of thundering hooves, the roaring of the men as they rode into battle, replaced now by the washing of the sleet on his face and mournful cries of the cold wind. He wished its howling might drown out the moaning of the injured men scattered all around, who had fought so bravely for him.

Full of remorse, Donal had spent the last few hours moving amongst the dying on the drenched and muddy battlefield, amidst the cries and pleas for help, offering what comfort he could. He made promises of care for families left behind in Beara, but the words had seemed so empty when he recognised those whom he had played with as a boy, or ridden with over wild landscapes on some mad adventure when they were young men. Their loved ones would have little to remember them by, and indeed no man had more than the clothes on his back, all of their possessions and supplies having been abandoned in the flight from the first camp. After all the careful planning, the earlier victories, he had never dreamed that it might come to this. With over a hundred and fifty men lost—more than a third of his Beara force, Donal was at a loss as to what his next move might be. Already the O'Mahonys, O'Driscolls and some of the MacCarthys had abandoned their camps and set off for home, carrying their injured men.

History would tell its own story, but Donal knew at least that neither he, nor any other southern chieftain, could be deemed culpable. They had objected to the idea of an outright attack, but in the end they had been forced to follow orders they knew to be flawed. The Spaniards would also, no doubt, be blamed but had not been at fault. They had after all been hemmed in at Kinsale for three months, without sufficient power or ordnance for diversionary assaults. As far as he was concerned the blame lay solely with O'Neill and that hothead, O'Donnell, their petty bickering and rivalry for victory over the Crown forces. It was no surprise that the English had heard of their plans and were anticipating their arrival; messengers had been dispatched to the various camps that spread out over a four-mile radius. Surely the birds in the air and the rats scurrying through the fields had known of the attack.

The sound of heavy boots wrenching a path through the mud brought Donal Cam to his feet, sword in hand. Through the smoke filled air he saw O'Neill approaching, accompanied by a few of the Munster chieftains. Surprised, he let the sword drop at his side. 'What are you doing here? I thought ye had all left.'

'O'Donnell went south, with some of his retinue. His brother is leaving now with what's left of their army, and heading back north' O'Neill replied with an edge of despair in his voice.

'And yourself?'

'I'll be moving northwards too, before the day is ended, but I want to tell you first that you are to take over as Commander in Chief of the southern forces.'

Donal was stunned, and paused for a moment before answering 'I am honoured, Hugh, but I have no knowledge or experience of commanding an entire army.'

'You cannot refuse' said O'Neill. 'There is no one else in Munster as powerful as you, or one who is held in such high regard.'

'Well then I thank you, Hugh, but my strengths are only a shadow of your own, you who gathered all the powers of Ireland together.'

One of Donal's men brought the last remains of the food and drink from the makeshift hide tent. The chieftains sat around the struggling fire and ate in silence, each consumed by their own thoughts. After a while Hugh looked up with a grim expression on his face. 'We were bloody fools, all of us.'

'Possibly', Donal replied.

'Surely we knew that it wouldn't work, trying to move ten thousand men through that roughest, darkest of nights. The devil himself would have lost his way. It was a miracle O'Donnell was looking for, and the glory for himself, and it nearly sent us all to our deaths. If we'd only have waited another week or two the English would have been starved into submission, and the glory would have been Ireland's own.'

'It's over now, Hugh; we must look to the future.'

'And look to you, Donal. The fight against Mountjoy and Carew down here is in your hands now.'

'But most of the southern chieftains have gone to defend their own territories; I don't know about the rest of the chieftains here.'

'They are all with you, Donal, they have given their word.'

'Well then, my friends, it's settled' said Donal, raising himself up as if in preparation for what lay ahead.

O'Neill nodded. 'As soon as I move out I will try to split Mountjoy's force by tempting him to follow me. You will then have only Carew's men to contend with, and though you may not be strong enough to give him battle in open country you should succeed in the wilds of West Cork. I'll give you Richard Tyrell and William Burke and their men; they are my two best captains, with experience in the field of battle. Only heed my warning against open battle.'

'I will, Hugh, thank you and God bless you.'

By late morning of Christmas Day, both Tyrell and Burke had arrived with their combined force of horsemen and foot soldiers. The other chieftains were summoned, and after prolonged discussion it was agreed that they would fight on as long as the Spanish commander, de Aquila, would commit himself to one last attack on the English rear. Mountjoy and Carew were celebrating their victory now, and it would be the last thing they were expecting. A letter was immediately dispatched, telling de Aquila of the plan to attack at daybreak the following morning.

The messenger returned just before nightfall with the Spanish commander's reply. Donal opened it and read aloud: '"Esteemed ally, my troops are weary and so am I. Our food is running out and I have lost many men to sickness. I believe our armies to be too small to mount a successful attack, and have therefore sued for peace. This is the only honourable path open to me, as any further assistance from Spain seems extremely doubtful. Your friend, Don Juan de Aquila."' Donal thrust the letter into the flames. 'That cowardly bastard, he's going to surrender to Mountjoy. There is no use in our remaining here. Without his help any offensive would be madness. We must return to Castlehaven, and await news of other assistance from Spain.'

Over in the English camp, Lord Mountjoy and Sir George Carew were indeed rejoicing in their unexpected victory. Only days ago they had been trapped between the Spaniards in Kinsale and the Irish surrounding, reduced to eating their own horses with over two thousand men deserted and another eight hundred dead of fever. Another week would have seen their surrender, but instead they had utterly defeated the superior rebel force and incurred the loss of less than twenty men. It had all been accomplished at the cost of a bottle of aqua vitae for a thirsty Irishman. The arrival of a letter from de Aquila, declaring his desire to surrender, was cause for further celebration, and the festivities continued well into the following morning, when the Spanish commander and all of his officers made their way into the camp under a flag of truce.

De Aquila was welcomed like a brother by Mountjoy, and he and all of his men were lavishly entertained during the following days and nights. New supplies arrived from England, and the surrender was negotiated at tables that could barely support their burden of food and drink. It was agreed that in return for giving up all of the Irish castles along the southwest coast—Castlehaven, Dunasead, Dunalong, Dun an Oir and Dunboy—the Spanish army would sail safely out of Kinsale, taking everything that they possessed.

They departed their new friends almost reluctantly, and Captains Harvey and Flower were duly dispatched by sea to Castlehaven, with three companies of troops, to take the castles. The weather was against them, however, and in the end they were forced to return to the shelter of Kinsale harbour to ride out the storm.

Donal was deeply involved in a discussion of future plans with Tyrell and Burke when his two younger sons, Donnell and Teige, returned from their foraging expedition.

'Well' enquired their father, 'How did ye do?'

'It's not too good; we have about twenty pigs and six cows ready for cleaning, the men have them over there at the big fire. At least it's something' Donnell replied.

'It is' Donal agreed. 'Now come here and meet Richard Tyrell, and William Burke. Their forces will join ours as we move west to Castlehaven.'

The men greeted one another, and then the planning continued. Donal enquired whether his sons had seen anything of their cousins, the Carriganass O'Sullivans, who had been behind them as they rode into battle.

'There has been no word from them, Father' Teige replied, 'But they may still be here.'

I think not' said Donal glumly. 'They are more likely to have returned to Carriganass, or else gone begging to Mountjoy for peace.' He rose and stretched his long limbs; 'If we're moving out tomorrow morning we need to find some carts, something to transport our injured and what supplies we have.'

'Come, Teige' said Donnell, and shouting for a few men the two young men remounted and disappeared from view in a matter of seconds.

'And us' Tyrell asked, 'What would you have us do?'

'I would like to know of the situation in the English camps.'

'Right, I'll go over with some men and scout around, and report back to you later.'

By early afternoon the rumbling of wheels could be heard in the distance, and soon Donal's sons appeared. 'Father' said Donnell breathlessly, 'We found six long carts, and four carriages. They must have been abandoned by O'Neill's men.'

'Well done, both of ye. Now we can pack up what we have left, and the wounded can be carried.' Hearing a horse Donal turned to see Captain Tyrell arrive and dismount. 'What's the news, Richard?'

'Red Hugh is to leave for Spain, in hope of some aid, and Hugh O'Neill is heading north.'

'And the English?'

'All quiet, Donal. There are two English ships anchored north along the coast, and they brought food and other supplies ashore this morning. No doubt they are still celebrating their victory.'

'And we are wasting our time here, my friend. We will move off for Castlehaven at first light, and await news from Spain. If there is none, we'll continue westwards to Dunboy, and prepare for the arrival of the English forces. It'll take them a good few weeks to venture west I think.'

Teige looked up at his father. 'And would we have the strength to hold out against them, when they come?'

'I don't know, Son. We would at least be fighting on our own ground, and on our own terms.'

Night fell early, the sky darkening again under the weight of another snow. Although his men had managed to make some improvements to the animal skin shelter, Donal preferred to stay outside and warm himself by the bright fire, before he went inside to rest in readiness for the long journey home. Watching the flames burn blue, the sparks leaping into the black night sky, he thought of his family back at Dunboy. They would be finishing their meal together in the great hall now, making their way up to their warm beds. Over at Ardea, where he had left her with their infant son, his cousin's wife, Ellen, would be in her chamber by the fire. Maybe she was in her nightclothes, loosening the braids in her luscious hair, glossy locks glowing in the light of the flames. For two years now he had known the heat of her lithe body next to his own, and he ached for it now, but it would be a week or more before he would be back in Beara. At least Ellen and the boy would be safe, well cared for by his uncle Philip; was he a fool to be risking his own life, when such precious people were waiting for him? Was he fit to take up this command when he had so little experience, would have to rely so much on the experience of Tyrell and Burke? But it was all decided now, Donal told himself as he rose and made his way into the tent, the outcome resting in the hands of fate.

Well before dawn Donal was woken from a fitful sleep and handed a dry piece of bread and a goblet of hot mead and brandy. Feeling the liquor burn down through his cold bones he was up, alert and ready to move. As the melancholy sound of the bull's horn filled the air he passed through the camp shouting instructions to his men, and as they rose like shadows in the half light it seemed as if the ground was coming alive. Mounting his horse, Donal Cam surveyed the scene as the rising sun revealed it in all its horror. The division of his army into their clan groups showed just how heavy the losses had been, and all around the injured were trying to raise themselves and each other; nobody wanted to die so far from home. Many resembled the walking dead themselves, and yet they struggled to lift their neighbours or their kin onto stretchers and carts. Men carried their brothers, uncles, fathers, sons. Of the two hundred Spanish soldiers that had come with him from Castlehaven, he could count only fifty-five.

Soon the carts were loaded, the men ready and the two captains at Donal's side. 'We must be on our way' he said. 'I don't want Carew to catch us in open country. Richard, you can ride ahead with a hundred men, and I'll send my two hundred best behind you on foot. Prepare the abbey at Bantry for attack, and then send half your force on to Dunboy to begin the preparations there. The castle was not built to withstand cannon fire, and the walls will need strengthening.'

'Very well, Donal' Tyrell replied. 'Is there a message for your family?'

'They should be told the truth of what happened, and that I will be there as soon as I can.'

Donal experienced a twinge as foreboding as he watched Tyrell and his men ride away, but he had to turn his attention to the present situation. Summoning his son Donell he said 'Yourself and Captain Burke here can go ahead with some men to the river crossing at Poolnalong, and make arrangements to have the boats ready for our crossing. I don't want to be stranded on the north bank with the English behind me. When you have crossed over yourselves, go out into O'Hea's and O'Cowhig's country and find food; beg or kill for it if you have to.'

Donal and his men arrived at Poolnalong some four hours later. Along the road that day more than twenty men died of their wounds, but rather than being buried by the wayside they were carried until the following day, when they reached the abbey at Timoleague. The monks gave each of them a full Christian burial and they were laid to rest in sacred ground, which would be of some comfort to their families at home. Donal could see that his army was weak and starving, and decided to encamp by a small river two miles south of the abbey. Just as he was dismounting his son and Captain Burke arrived, bearing cattle, sheep, and four cartloads of grain and other supplies.

Fires were quickly laid, and the animals jointed and thrown on them to roast. The ravenous men could hardly wait to lay their hands on the hot, bloody meat, and Donal himself was surprised by the ferocity of his hunger as he tore into a lump of mutton. Before he had finished his meal however, a shout went up that riders were approaching. A call to arms was sounded throughout the camp, and all food was thrown aside for the moment.

Donal's fears of a surprise English attack faded fast, as he recognised some members of the O'Hurley clan from Ballinacarriga riding in. They numbered about fifty in all, and Donal was astonished to see that four of them were women, wearing the same mail as their fellow soldiers. He recalled then that the O'Hurley women were well known for going into battle with their menfolk, but he had never witnessed it before.

As they reined up, he shouted 'Ye are welcome to join us, and to anything we have.'

'Thank you, my friend' said Randal Oge O'Hurley as he walked towards him. 'We have our own supplies, but will rest here awhile if we may, before we continue on our journey home.'

The two men embraced like brothers, and then sat down together by the roaring fire with meat and drink. Very soon the conversation turned to the battle. 'Tell me' said Donal, 'What did you see of it?'

'I saw that it was a disaster. That idiot O'Donnell should be hanged. When dawn was breaking some of our own men were attacked on the north flank by O'Neill's forces, who had mistaken them for Mountjoy's army in the poor light. The bloody fools should have been a mile further south. I lost twenty of my best men in that skirmish, including a first cousin, Cathal.'

'Ah, so that's what happened. O'Neill didn't tell me that.'

'I don't suppose he did, Donal. We were nearly cut off as we were coming up behind you. Still, it's over now. What are your plans?'

'The Spaniards have surrendered, so we are on our way to Castlehaven to wait for aid, or even some arms. O'Donnell has left there by now and is sailed for Spain himself.'

'My men are at your disposal when you're ready, my friend; I will be waiting to hear from you.'

'Thank you, Randal. I'll send word whatever occurs.'

By this time a small crowd had gathered around the four women, who had dismounted and were removing their Norman style armour. Donal raised an eyebrow, asking 'Are those women your kin, Randal?'

'They are, and they fight as well as any man on the battlefield.' Randal Oge called the women over and introduced them individually. 'This is my sister Helen, and these my cousins, Esther, Julia and Johanna, who are as yet unmarried.' With a laugh, he went on 'The wild ones, we call them, and can't get any man to take them. They are too strong willed to take orders from a husband.'

The women shook Donal by the hand in turn, and silently he admired the power in each of their grasps. Turning back to Randal he smiled 'A few years ago I would have taken my chances here.'

'Ah no, Donal Cam' Randal replied, slapping his friend on the back, 'I won't believe that your fire is out yet. But from what I hear you've enough on your hands at home!'

The two men continued their blustering, and hardly noticed that Donnell and Teige, accompanied by two of their friends, had introduced themselves to the O'Hurley women and that all of them were drifting towards another fire, and out of sight.

An hour or more had passed, and Donal began to look around for his sons, and then sent a servant to search for them. He didn't want them getting involved with any young women at this point, especially not the O'Hurleys, as he had already made up his mind that they should sail for Spain on the first available ship. His family had suffered enough losses in his lifetime, and he wanted his heirs out of Ireland now, until the fighting was over.

Randal noted his concern. 'They are two fine boys you have, Donal.'

'They are, and I know what you have in mind Randal, but the time isn't right. We might be in a better position to arrange some marriages in the future; they are young enough to wait for peace.'

'I suppose you're right. Yourself and your sons are always welcome at Ballinacarriga anyway. And despite her strange ways and regal airs, Catherine's hospitality is generous.'

The servant returned and reported that he had been unable to find Donnell or Teige, and Donal grew alarmed, fearing that they had wandered, unarmed, outside of the camp. Six of his personal guards were dispatched, and soon found all of the young people in an isolated hay barn belonging to the neighbouring O'Heas. They had paired off and were lying in various states of undress, engaged in varying degrees of intimacy, beside discarded items of clothing and empty wine jugs. Their visitors were simply ignored, until one of them spoke. 'Your father sent us to find you. You are to return to the camp.'

Donnell struggled to disentangle himself from the naked woman on top of him, who leapt to her feet without shame and laughed. 'Ah, why not tell Donal Cam that you were unable to find us; we're only enjoying these prize stallions here.'

'I'm sorry' replied the guard, who was having trouble controlling his own features, 'But we cannot return without the master's sons.'

There was clearly no use in arguing, and the revellers stumbled to their feet, found their clothes, and did their best to exit the barn with some dignity.

Donal was furious to see his sons being escorted back to the camp in a state of such inebriation and disarray, singing as if they had no concerns at all. 'What do ye think ye're about?'

'Nothing, Father' Donnell replied with a hiccup. 'Only a little fun. Didn't we need it after these weeks of battle and hardship? After all, we are our father's sons.'

Donal's jaw was clenched tight. 'I should have you horse-whipped for talking to me like that. Now get to your tent, and out of my sight.'

Although he was exhausted, Donal got no sleep that night. Two of his men, with whom he had been close, were dying. One had been shot in the stomach, another had lost a hand, and they could not be saved. They gave up the fight just as dawn was breaking, and were buried with their colleagues in the cold earth of the abbey grounds, before the army set off westwards once more.

Chapter Two

The Journey Westward

With their hunger at least partially satisfied, the army marched quickly. Urged on by Donal they were moving almost at a run, and covered the first ten miles in record time. Avoiding Rosscarbery, which had been an English stronghold, they headed for the Leap. Nobody could ignore the hastily dug graves with their rough timber crosses, or the stench of the unburied bodies lying along the trail. Clearly there were many men struggling to reach their homes before death overcame them.

It was Donal's intention to make camp that night under the battlements of Castle Iomhair, which wasn't far from Castlehaven. He rode alongside his two sons, but at no point did he address himself directly to them. He was still furious about their foolish escapade of the previous night, which had endangered their lives and embarrassed Donal himself. His thoughts turned then to the local chieftain Tadhg O'Donovan, as he realised that there had been no sign of him either leading up to or during the Kinsale battle. Tadhg, of course, might well have been lurking in the shadows, waiting for an opportune moment to make his presence felt; they said he took after his famous ancestor, Ivor O'Donovan, the wily magician and pirate chief who became the scourge of the southwest coast. Ivor probably had Spanish ancestry, and his dark features earned him the name of an Giolla Roebach, the Swarthy Warrior. He had been poisoned by his own cousins, and was said to have sworn, with his dying breath, that he would return to haunt his murderers. Donal knew well the legend telling of the annual appearance of Ivor's ship, under full sail and with guns blasting, on Lake Cluhir, which was just a mile below the walls of Castle Iomhair.

Night was falling when the leading column approached Iomhair. Donal called two of his riders aside and gave them instructions to ride ahead to Castlehaven. He wanted them to find out if there were any Spanish ships at anchor or any news of aid, and report back to him when he reached the O'Donovan castle. As he set off again to cover the last mile, Donal's mind wandered back to the last time he had arrived in Castlehaven, a few weeks earlier, just in time to prevent another disaster.

Having heard that the Spaniards had landed and were in urgent need of his assistance, Donal had force marched his small army from Beara in just over twenty-four hours. Hearing gun and cannon fire in the distance he had ridden ahead with six of his men and seen the disembarkation of English troops from a number of ships on the shoreline. He had given the order to attack, and while a hundred of his horsemen swam across the narrows near Raheen Castle to help the Spaniards defend their gun placements, he sent the rest of his men roaring and screaming through the woods, towards the hastily drawn English lines.

Fearing that they were under attack from a vastly superior force, the English troops had abandoned their positions immediately and rushed back along the rocky shore to their boats, suffering severe losses along the way. With not one single man lost on his own side, Donal had thought at the time that the victory augured well for the coming engagement at Kinsale, but sadly he had been proved wrong.

Donal had ridden then into the castle at Castlehaven, where the O'Driscoll brothers received him. The Spanish commander, Don Zubiaur, hailed him as a saviour while the cannons on the English ships in the harbour fell around them. He had been concerned, however, for the Spanish gunners on the opposite side of the harbour. After two of their transporters had been driven ashore to facilitate the offloading of cannons, they had come under heavy bombardment from the English ships.

Over a hundred Spanish troops and two hundred Irish had quickly been sent across the water on small boats, to strengthen the embattled garrison. Later, when gale force winds had prevented the English ships from leaving the harbour, they were subjected to a bombardment from the guns under the castle and those on the Point opposite. All their manoeuvres were in vain, and they were easy targets in the enclosed inlet, until they launched their longboats and slowly towed the ships out of the harbour to catch a favourable wind. The ships, which included the Warspite, Defiance, Swiftsure and Marlin and were under the command of Admiral Levison, had all incurred serious damage, and more than five hundred men had been wounded or killed.

When they reached Castle Iomhair on this day, Donal and the other chieftains were greeted with open arms by Cathal O'Donovan. He led them into the great hall, where a feast was quickly being laid down. Cathal had not been seen during the recent battle, but now that they were availing themselves of his generous hospitality, his guests thought it wiser not to demand an explanation. He would offer them one in his own time.

The men ate their fill, and were enjoying some fine Spanish wine and Cathal's own mead when he rose to toast the valour of his visitors at Kinsale. 'I know you will be curious' he said at last, 'About my own absence from the battle. The truth is that when I saw Donal here marching eastward with his powerful army, I decided that the few men that I could muster would be better employed here, strengthening the castle. You may think it a selfish decision, but I do believe that my presence in Kinsale would have made no difference at all to the final outcome. At least I can offer you and all of your men my hospitality now.'

A pregnant silence ensued, which was broken by Donal. Standing, he lifted his goblet and said 'To our noble host, who has welcomed us like a brother. May God strengthen all of us in the days that lie ahead.'

The deafening applause, shouting and table thumping that followed this exchange grew louder still when a large group of young women were ushered into the hall. Huge jugs of brandy and poteen were brought to the table as the musicians began to play, and the women joined the men in their drinking. Some of them began to undress and step up on the long tables to dance, and soon all memories of the bitter defeat were drowned as the warriors wallowed in an orgy of debauchery.

Dawn brought a different story. Con O'Driscoll of Castlehaven arrived with Donal's two messengers and some sobering news. A spy who had been left behind in Kinsale had ridden through the night to inform them that Don Juan de Aquila had surrendered all of the Irish castles that had been occupied by the Spaniards. Cathal O'Donovan went with Donnell and Teige to search the dark chambers for their father. They found him eventually under some furs, wrapped around the body of a naked young woman.

'Wake up, Father' Donnell shook him until he lifted his head. 'We have bad news.'

Donal groaned weakly. 'What . . . what is it? Oh my bloody head. What are you saying?'

'Aquila has surrendered all the castles on the southwest coast to Mountjoy, including your own.'

Donal leapt to his feet and began dressing himself furiously. 'That cursed coward! Never will I allow the English to lay their hands on Dunboy, never!' Pulling on his armour with the aid of a bleary-eyed servant he strode out of the chamber, roaring for his horse to be saddled. As he emerged into the open air he thought he heard cannon fire, and looking towards the lake his fevered mind apprehended the dim outline of a ship under full sail. Rubbing his sore eyes, he looked again; there was nothing there. Recalling the legend of Ivor O'Donovan's ghost ship he hurried on, trying to dismiss the notion that what he had seen was a bad omen.

Within the hour the army was on the move once more. Donal took a hundred and fifty men with him towards Castlehaven, while William Burke took the rest and headed for Bantry. Donal's main objective was to throw the Spaniards out of Castlehaven, but not before he had seen their ship sailing out of the harbour with his two sons aboard. He could only hope that the Spanish garrison remained ignorant of the terms of de Aquila's surrender.

From the top of the hill Donal was relieved to see the Spanish ship still riding at anchor, and an absence of any English sails on the horizon. There would be no further confrontation for the moment, and maybe the gods were looking favourably upon his endeavours again.

When he arrived at Castlehaven Donal was greeted by Con O'Driscoll's brothers, who showed him to their upper chamber. 'You have heard the news' said Donagh. 'What are we going to do?'

'Do the Spaniards here know anything?'

'They do not, thanks be to God.'

'And that Spanish panache, when does she sail?'

'On the tide, in about two hours.'

'Have any of our allies gone aboard?'

'Only Red Hugh; he went to secure a cabin for the voyage to Spain.'

'And he has not returned?'

'He will be back soon, Donal. His belongings and his servants are still here in the castle.'

'Let me know when he returns, will you? I have a few words to say to that man. Meanwhile, I must write a letter to the King of Spain.'

Writing swiftly in Latin, Donal outlined recent events and informed the King that he would hold onto Dunboy at all costs. He added that he was sending his sons to Spain and placing them under his protection, but made no mention of his plans for the Spanish garrisons. When the letter was finished, he sent for Donnell and Teige. 'Listen carefully boys' he said as he sat back in his chair. 'You are to take that ship for Spain, as a matter of your own protection. I have written to King Philip and will send word also to the Duke of Cáceras, and you will be well taken care of. If the situation here worsens, myself and the rest of the family can join you there.'

Teige nodded. 'And now, Father?'

'Now I will go west, and hold Dunboy until another Spanish fleet arrives. You had better go and organise clothing and supplies for your voyage.'

Donal entered the great hall just as Hugh O'Donnell arrived back. Greeting him without warmth, Donal enquired about the purpose of his voyage to Spain.

'You know well' Hugh replied, 'That I go to petition the King to send another fleet.'

'Are you serious? After what you did at Kinsale?'

'What the hell do you mean, Donal?'

'I mean your foolish, impetuous attack; your assault on O'Neill's flank instead of the English front line. You were responsible for our defeat.'

O'Donnell's face darkened. 'You're wrong, God damn it you're wrong!'

'You know that I am right. Now I will have to try and repair some of the damage, while your brother and O'Neill take most of the remaining Irish force and head north.'

Raging, O'Donnell drew his sword and lunged at Donal, shouting 'I am not to blame!'

Donal stepped aside, and released his own sword. The clash of metal on metal echoed throughout the castle as each of the men sought to gain the upper hand. Donal was the better swordsman however, and parried Red Hugh's lunges and downward strokes until with one swift movement he struck his opponents sword at the handle, and sent it spinning across the room. Resisting this further disgrace, Hugh pulled his dagger and roared 'Come then, my friend, try and kill me now!'

Donal let his sword drop at his side. 'Enough Irish blood has been spilt already, and I don't want yours on my hands. Go to Spain, see what you can do.'

The time had come for Donnell and Teige to board the ship to Spain, and Donal came to take his leave of them with a troubled expression on his face. 'Conditions will be crowded' he advised them, 'And you will suffer sickness when you're out at sea'.

'Don't worry Father' said Donnell. 'You forget that we have both been to sea before. And Donagh O'Driscoll will be making the voyage with us, and has undertaken to offer any help or advice that we might need.'

'That's good, Donnell. Perhaps the three of you can convince King Philip to help us; I don't have much faith in Hugh O'Donnell.'

'We'll do whatever we can', Teige assured him. The young men embraced their father in turn, each of them aware that they might never see one another again.

'Take care, Father' Donnell added with a hint of sadness in his voice.

'You need not worry about me, Son. Don't you remember what the old hag of Beara said to me once? That I would die suddenly, on foreign soil. Now I bid you both farewell, and a safe voyage.'

The Spanish ship sailed out of the harbour just before nightfall. Donal was anxious to continue westward, so the O'Driscolls decided that they would wait a day or two before reclaiming their castle from the remaining Spanish garrison. Donal made no objections, but impressed upon them that they should act before the English arrived, and in the meantime train their best men to use the Spanish cannons.

The allied chieftains met up with the main body of the army some time after dark. Daniel MacCarthy and Connor of Kerry had decided to march through the night so as to arrive back in Kerry the following evening. They vowed to answer Donal's call at any time, coming to his aid with their combined force of fifteen hundred men. Donal pressed on, to Dunboy.

Until this time, Captain Tyrell and his men had been in occupation of the Franciscan monastery at Bantry. They had been somewhat disconcerted upon their arrival, when they were met with the sight of scantily clothed young women scattering like startled birds. Friar Jacobus had finally appeared, his face flushed and his expression flustered. 'Welcome, Captain Tyrell' he blustered.

'Thank you, Father' Tyrell replied with a wry smile. 'Might I ask what those females were doing here?'

'We choose to observe the old rites of the church, Captain. On one night of the year, each of us is allowed the company of a woman. I hope you do not disapprove?'

'Not at all' Tyrell replied, shaking his head in wonder, 'Not at all.'

The monks were objecting bitterly to the fortifications, maintaining a continuous prayer vigil as the tower and steeple were pulled down and the stones used for the exterior wall defences. Food and supplies had been brought in and stored in the cellars, in case of a siege situation, and boats had been drawn up on the north beach to facilitate an escape at any time. It was only now a matter of waiting for Donal's arrival, and keeping the restless men away from the vast quantities of wine and spirits that lay in the large cellar. The abbey was well known throughout Ireland as one of the greatest smuggling bases on the southwest coast.

Donal arrived in Bantry to hear that his cousin Owen had returned to Carriganass from Kinsale. Before going over to Reenavanny Castle, on Whiddy Island, he sent Tyrell to talk to Sir Owen, and ask him to meet with Donal and discuss the possibility of their joining forces. The Captain returned with the news that, although he had himself been cordially received, Owen would have nothing to do with his cousin, and had already successfully sued for peace. He had no intention of helping Donal fight what he regarded as a lost cause.

It was not a surprising response. Owen had ceased all contact with his cousin ever since his wife, Ellen, had left for the relative safety of Ardea Castle. The last thing she told him before he left for Kinsale was that she would never return to the misery and dampness of Carriganass, or to her husband's fits of rage. Her main concern, she told him, was now the infant that Donal had sired.

When Donal returned to the mainland he went to talk with Friar Jacobus, and advised him that the monks should leave immediately. Their lives could not be guaranteed if the abbey was attacked. The Friar was concerned about the huge stores of wine and other goods, but Donal swore that his men would guard them as well as they were able. 'If the English capture the place' he went on, 'I will make sure that every cask is broken open before they can lay their hands on it. Some of it, meanwhile, can be transferred to Reenavanny.'

The Friar sighed dejectedly as he went to summon the monks. 'God's will be done' he said.

As he watched the group of twelve monks leaving for Timoleague, Donal thought about the first time he had ever laid eyes on his Ellen at Carriganass. He was already married then, his wife also being called Ellen, but her beauty had enthralled him. She stood over five feet ten inches, with a fine figure, deep brown eyes and rich dark hair. Indeed, Ellen was renowned all over Munster and envied by all the chieftain's daughters. Donal was anxious to return to her and the boy, but first he must take Carriganass, a task which he hoped would consume only a day or two.

Owen O'Sullivan was taken completely by surprise when, on the morning of February eighth he found his castle surrounded by Donal's army. He organised his defences immediately, placing over eighty men armed with muskets on the walls, and waited for Donal to approach.

Riding up to the main gate alone, Donal called for Owen, and after a few moments he appeared on the wall and shouted 'What are you doing? I've no intention of surrendering my castle to you.'

'Don't be foolish' Donal replied. 'You can't hold out here, and we've had enough bloodshed.'

'Go home, Donal. Carew has already sent armaments, and is on his way here now; you have no cannons, no demi-culverins, it's hopeless.'

'I will not go home yet, Cousin. And if you believe that you're going to keep Carriganass for Carew, then you are wrong. I will return.'

Donal waited for four days, hoping that Owen might change his mind, but he knew that Carew might soon be in the area and on the morning of the twelfth he launched his attack. A battering ram, called a sow, had already been mounted on a large cart along with numerous timber ladders for the assault on the walls.

While musket fire was being concentrated on the walls and battlements, the sow was manoeuvred into place. After four rammings the big gates collapsed, providing the signal for the walls to be attacked. Just over two hours later Owen surrendered, and Donal allowed him and his men to leave for Macroom Castle; he had no appetite for further hostilities.

In the main chamber of the tower house, Donal sat down with his companions that afternoon to plan their rearguard action. Turning to Richard Tyrell, he enquired 'How long can this place and the abbey hold out?'

'The abbey won't cope with a long siege; if it is subjected to cannon fire it won't last more than a couple of days. As for this castle, I think we could hold out for a week with about two hundred armed men.'

'Right, Richard, you can take care of the defences, but I don't want to lose too many men. Don't give up without a struggle, but abandon both if it becomes necessary.'

Captain Burke enquired 'What can I do, Donal?'

'You can come west with me, and be ready to return when Richard needs you.'

'Would it not be better if I stayed here now?'

'I don't think so, William; you'll only be four hours away at the most.'

They were about to leave the chamber when one of Donal's

men rushed in with a message from the O'Driscolls. Fineen O'Driscoll had sent word that Captains Harvey and Flower had arrived in Castlehaven, and taken the castle after a struggle. They had gone on to Baltimore and overcome the defensive forces there, forcing them to sue for peace. It was the worst possible news. Now all of West Cork was at the mercy of the English, and no doubt they had set their sights on Dunboy. There was no time to be lost, and within the hour Donal's army was on the move, marching into a setting sun.

Chapter Three

Dunboy Castle

As darkness enveloped the landscape, Donal sent scouts ahead to find out whether the English might reach Dunboy before him. He was relieved to find that all was quiet at the castle, and there were no English ships in the harbour. Still fearing that the enemy might arrive at dawn, Donal urged his weary men on. The main bulk of his army were told to increase their speed, leaving the carts and carriages to follow at their own pace.

They arrived at Castledermot in the pale light of the early dawn, and Donal made his way into the castle and up the narrow stairway to the vantage point at the top of the tower. The entire harbour spread out before him, with Dunboy beyond, and he thanked God that he wasn't too late. There were no ship's lanterns to be seen, and only the glimmer of the castle fires; the gales of recent days must have prevented the English making the passage around the coast.

Leaving two men to keep watch, Donal returned to his men and ordered half of them to go home to their families. He planned to take up temporary residence at Castledermot, and kept two hundred and fifty with him, along with fifty horses; he would need them if he was obliged to throw the Spanish out of Dunboy by force.

Over a week earlier, Captain Harvey and Captain Flower had arrived in Castlehaven with a thousand troops on board six ships.

They were met with the sight of the Spaniards, under the command of Pedro de Soto, trying to regain the castle at Castlehaven. De Soto had finally been informed of the conditions of de Aquila's surrender, but was unwilling to give up so easily. When the English ships began to take up their positions however, and the troops to disembark, he agreed to a meeting with the two captains and the O'Driscoll brothers. Eventually the castle was surrendered without a fight, and an English garrison installed. De Soto then sailed with Harvey and Flower to Baltimore, where the castles of Dunalong and Dunasead were also handed over.

Exhilarated by his success Captain Harvey departed Baltimore with three ships, bound for Dunboy. Fortunately for Donal Cam the weather deteriorated further, into a full-blown storm. Two hundred men were swept overboard from the three ships, which limped back into Baltimore harbour.

Donal sent word to his uncle Dermod that he had arrived, but that the Spanish garrison must not learn of his presence as it was his intention to regain the castle. He also dispatched a messenger to Ellen at Ardea, before riding out to take a look at the work that had been done to reinforce his castle's walls and battlements. Dermod was already waiting for him at Castledermot when he returned, glad to see his nephew safe and well but concerned that his own castle on Oilean Beag was not defended.

'I know, Dermod, and I will make arrangements as soon as Dunboy is back in my hands. Fifty or sixty of my men will go west with you, and some of the small cannons; when the castle is ready I want you to take Ellen there, and guard her with your life.'

Later that evening Ellen herself arrived, and after a lengthy embrace the couple sat down to savour their time alone. Donal told her of his plans regarding Dursey, and she delighted him with news of their son's intelligence and agility. When the time came for Donal to sit down with his colleagues, Ellen made her excuses. William Burke had angered her straight away by looking her up and down as if she were a harlot, and she decided to go to Donal's bed chamber and await him there.

The chamber was lit only by the amber glow of the brazier, and Donal cursed quietly as he stumbled making his entrance. He hadn't drunk much that evening but a lack of sleep was beginning to catch up with him. No amount of exhaustion, however, could prevent him from almost trembling with anticipation as he made out Ellen's naked form, reclining on the fine feather bed. Throwing off his clothes he slipped under the skins and pulled her into his arms, kissing her hot flesh hungrily.

Ellen reached down for Donal's cock, surprised by how big and hard it seemed. She sat up astride him and guided it inside her, letting the rhythm of their movements merge and then build up while he reached up for the firm flesh of her breasts. As soon as she felt the delicious shuddering of a climax course through her loins, he exploded inside her and the two of them collapsed onto the bed. Stretching out beside his long body, Ellen took Donal's face in her hand and kissed his lips, whispering 'That was the best we've ever had.'

The knocking at the door came too soon for Ellen, who hung on to Donal's neck begging him not to leave her. They had only slept for a couple of hours, and the moon was still high in the sky. Disentangling himself gently, Donal kissed her hand. 'I have to go, woman, but we will be together again soon I promise you.'

The Spanish officers were unconcerned by the sight of Donal arriving at Dunboy with William Burke and twelve men just before dawn. They had no idea that two hundred men were at that moment quietly taking over the walls, the gate, and the bawn enclosure. Juan Garcia, the officer in charge, greeted Donal with great warmth. 'Welcome, my friend. I hope that you are in good health and did not suffer any injuries at Kinsale. What news do you bring?'

'You are aware of Don Juan de Aquila's surrender to the English?'

'I am, but that is all I know. Are we to leave now? When will our ships arrive?'

'Unfortunately I have had no contact with de Aquila. He has been enjoying the hospitality of the English' Donal replied, with some sarcasm in his tone. 'But I can tell you that we have to hold this castle until more help arrives from Spain.'

'And if the English get here first?'

'We will prepare for that possibility, but first I must take control here. I have been declared Commander in Chief of the Irish forces.'

Garcia's expression hardened. 'My orders are to hold this castle for King Philip.'

'Everything has changed. I order you and your men to hand over your arms and submit to my authority.'

'I am sorry, but until I receive direct orders from Spain, I will not relinquish control.'

The battle was sudden and fierce. Shots filled the air and men fought hand to hand with swords and daggers. Somehow Donal escaped injury, but Dermod's son Ciaran and two other youths from Dursey fell mortally wounded. They were completely outnumbered until the arrival of those who had come over the walls. Seeing their companions scattered dead or bleeding on the ground, they launched a ferocious attack that Donal had to curtail. 'Enough' he roared. 'There will be enough killing when the English come. Now take those Spanish bastards away, they'll be hanged at daybreak.'

William Burke was at his side in an instant. 'Do you not think' he enquired, 'That the Spanish gunners would be more use to us alive? Our priority is to defend the castle.'

'I suppose you're right' Donal replied grudgingly. 'Let them go to the dungeon instead.'

Later that day, when Donal was reinstalled at Dunboy, a rider arrived with a message from Hugh O'Neill. It read: 'My friend, I have suffered heavy losses on my march northwards. My carriages and carts and two hundred men were lost as we crossed the

Shannon. We were attacked from all sides, and by the time I reached my own territory I had lost over a thousand men at the hands of my fellow Irishmen.'

Donal was not surprised by the news; he had heard how O'Neill and O'Donnell had plundered and slaughtered during their march to Kinsale. At any rate he expected no further help from the northern allies, and Carew would be here any day now over land or sea. Looking up at the exhausted messenger he made no response, but only asked him his name.

'I am Sean O'Rourke, my lord.'

'Well, Sean, go and get some food and rest. Your horse will be taken care of and you can return when you are fit again.'

Two days later, Donal rode east with twenty men to visit Tyrell at his camp at Ardnagashel. He knew of the captain's dislike of confined spaces, and was less surprised by his decision to camp out with the men than by the splendour of his tent. Numerous cowhides formed a watertight canopy over a carpet of sheepskins, which rested on a thick bed of straw. 'You have a fine shelter here Richard', said Donal by way of greeting.

'Better anyway than cold castle walls, oozing water' he replied. 'I have sent for my wife and some close relations.'

'They would be welcome at Dunboy.'

'No thank you, Donal, although I have heard of the many comforts of your grand castle. I would prefer to have them here with me.'

'As you wish. Now tell me about the defences at Carriganass.'

'Our position there is weak, Donal. Even if we could prevent the English crossing the river, they could soon take it with cannon-fire.'

'Carriganass stands at the gateway to the west, and the north into Desmond, Richard; we need to hold it.'

'Then we will do our best, Donal, as ever.'

That night brought little respite, as a rider came in from the O'Driscolls to say that Harvey and Flower had installed large garrisons in Castlehaven and Baltimore, and were making sorties out into the countryside destroying all the crops. It was only a matter of time until they marched westward. Tyrell immediately dispatched two pairs of scouts, with instructions to report any movement in their direction.

Donal returned to Dunboy, and three days later Captain Flower arrived in Bantry with some six hundred foot soldiers and a hundred horses. As Captain Tyrell raced to the abbey with an increased force of one hundred and twenty men, Flower was already positioning a number of cannons, overlooking them to the south. The abbey was pounded all of that day and well into a second, before a ground attack was launched. The defence was a valiant one, and Tyrell repelled the English on several occasions, but at a cost. Thirty-five men were killed and another twenty or so wounded. Four nights into the assault he decided that the abbey wasn't worth the loss of any more lives. Remembering Donal's instructions he went to the cellar with a few men. After removing a dozen small casks of brandy they broke every remaining vessel open with their axes; the floor was awash and the heady aroma of wine and spirits permeated the entire abbey.

Carrying their injured amongst them the defending force made their way out of the grounds in the darkness, filing down into the small boats they had left ready. Landing at Donemark they headed for Carriganass, while a rider was sent to inform Donal of the events.

Very soon, Tyrell received reports that the abbey was being rebuilt as a fortress, and that a diamond shaped battlement was being dug out on top of the hill to the south. It indicated that Flower intended to stay in the area, and he decided to make a few sudden night attacks. These at least were effective, in that they prevented the English from advancing any further; but the situation was about to grow far more serious.

In early March of 1601 Lord Mountjoy instructed the Earl of Thomond to go in to West Cork with two and a half thousand men. He was to burn all the crops, round up the cattle and root out and destroy the rebels. On his way west he strengthened

Captain Harvey's force in Baltimore by about five hundred, and briefly laid siege to the castle at Kilcoe. The MacCarthy's defences were, however, impregnable and he marched on, reaching Bantry by the end of the month. Captain Flower advised him of the ongoing fortification of Dunboy Castle, and so the decision was taken to arrive there as soon as possible.

Richard Tyrell had other ideas for Thomond's forces. Aware that he was utterly outnumbered he left only a token force at Carriganass itself, but arranged them so that the castle appeared to be fully defended. Keeping his horsemen in reserve, he deployed the rest of his men in the nearby woods. The English arrived at the south side of the river and placed their cannons. As they opened fire they attempted to cross, but musket men hiding in the trees picked them off as they appeared. The tactic worked well for over four days, until additional cannons were drawn up and began to fire randomly into the woods. Tyrell's men were dislodged, and many of them injured or killed; the castle was abandoned, and Tyrell forced to retreat to the dense forest lining the Coomhola River. There, he waited for the advancing columns.

After two days, a number of companies crossed the Ouvane and approached the Coomhola inlet without encountering any opposition. But as soon as they entered the deep woods they were attacked from all sides. Six hours later the English were retreating, and were harried all the way back to the Ouvane River. The balance had shifted, and Tyrell exploited the new situation mercilessly; almost four hundred were left for dead in the woods, and the river ran red.

Thomond summoned his officers for a council of war, and told them that he would now be leading the troops personally. It made no difference, as the following two attempts to march west failed and they were forced to retreat on both occasions. There were many more English soldiers lost, and Thomond was lucky to escape with his life. Disheartened, he left four companies to hold Whiddy island and Reenavanny Castle, another two hundred men at Carriganass, and turned back to Cork to seek reinforcements.

Captains Tyrell and Burke, meanwhile, were pleased with their success but angered by Donal's absence. If he had brought his own men in even greater losses might have been inflicted, and any further plans on the part of the English curtailed. Tyrell believed that the chance of a total defeat of Thomond's army had been missed.

Riding swiftly to Dunboy, Tyrell was met by Donal's eldest son, Dermod, and asked him where his father might be.

'My lord, my father is at Ardea Castle. He has moved his army over there while he awaits the Spanish fleet.'

'And what of his castle here; shouldn't he be looking after the fortifications?'

'You must ask him about that' Dermod replied a little sullenly.

'I suppose he has his woman with him?'

'I suppose he does. They left together, to see the child.'

'And I am left to do all of his defending for him.'

'As I said, Captain, you had better talk to him.'

Tyrell rode away thinking that Donal had a very arrogant son; the poor fool would soon learn if the English came west. As for himself, his only action was to send a message to Donal. It informed him that if he was not at the base at Glengarriff woods by the following night, Tyrell would gather up his forces and head back up north to join O'Neill.

The following afternoon Donal duly arrived at the base, but he was seething with anger at being summoned in such a manner. 'What is this talk of heading north' he blustered as he dismounted.

'Well, I understood that you were more interested in your cousin's wife than defending your property.'

'Don't talk to me in that manner. I went to Ardea to inspect the defences, and took Ellen with me for safety. The Spaniards know the bay there anyway, and will send their ships there first.'

'To hell with the Spaniards, we don't need them; if you had joined us in Bantry we could have destroyed Thomond's forces while I had them on the rack.'

'By the time I got your message I was already at Ardea, and the torrential rain stopped us returning over the mountains. Richard, this fighting between ourselves can only harm our cause. Let us sit down together and make our plans as allies.'

Tyrell relented a little, seeing the truth in Donal's words. 'As you wish, my friend.'

Chapter Four

False Rumours

When Thomond arrived in Cork he was informed that Sir George Carew, the Lord President of Munster, had joined his army at their temporary quarters in Inniscara. Taking three of his officers, Thomond rode the short journey to present himself to his superior there.

Carew offered no welcome, and his face remained fixed in a frown. 'What in the name of God happened?'

'I am sorry, my lord. Although we made three attempts we were unable to reach Dunboy from Bantry; the rebels held the woods, and we lost over eight hundred men.'

Standing up Carew faced his visitor, his face reddening with anger. 'How could you have lost so many? It is not possible!'

'These are no ordinary rebels, my lord. They are skilled tacticians, with Tyrell and Burke leading them, and they are brave. In the woods and forests at least they have an advantage.'

'I see; well I must send to Mountjoy with this news, and then I will take the troops to Dunboy myself. That last stronghold must be taken at all costs.'

'Whatever you say, my lord' said Thomond, bowing.

'Now return to what's left of your men, and await my instructions.'

Mountjoy gave his permission for all of the English and allied forces in Munster to be brought together, and Carew prepared to march them west and meet him there. Sir George was looking forward to this opportunity to prove himself as a leader, which might gain him promotion and so a passage out of Ireland. He was extremely frustrated, therefore, when only two thousand foot soldiers and two hundred horses materialised, and knew that his action had been compromised. There was no option but to set off anyway, and Carew knew that he had seven hundred men in Bantry, and could call on the resources of the O'Donovans and Owen O'Sullivan. He marched out of Cork on the twenty-third of April, 1601.

The army camped at the Owenboy River near Kinsale that night, and arrived the following evening at Timoleague. Another night was spent at Rosscarbery, and on the following day Carew broke off to see Captain Harvey at Castlehaven. Noting that there were two English ships in the harbour, and more than enough men to hold the castle, Carew took two hundred foot soldiers with him as he left to rejoin the main force. When they were encamped at Oldcourt, near Baltimore, Sir George went to ensure that the defences of Dunasead and Dunalong would withstand fresh attacks should a Spanish fleet arrive. Kinsale, he knew, was handsomely protected.

The Irish allies under the Earl of Thomond and Lord Percy had by this time reinforced Carew's army. They discussed the possibility of an assault on Kilcoe, which was still being held by the MacCarthys, but decided that they couldn't afford to engage in a lengthy siege at this point. They pressed on to Bantry, where a camp was finally established close to the ruins of an old castle at Donemark, which bore Carew's family name. He had heard that Fineen MacCarthy had razed it, in 1261. There they were joined by Owen O'Sullivan, with fifty foot soldiers and twenty horsemen. Carew knew something of Sir Owen's dispute with his cousin Donal Cam, and enquired as to his feelings about the regaining of Carriganass.

'I will be forever in your debt' Owen replied, 'For the recapture of my property, and will be happy to help you now in any way that I am able.'

Carew summoned his officers and then they conversed for more than four hours, with O'Sullivan offering up valuable information regarding Dunboy and its defences, and the strength and locations of Donal's forces. It became clear that the combined forces of the rebels roughly matched their own, but that Tyrell would be able to muster hundreds of additional horsemen in a matter of hours. It would almost certainly be necessary, Carew decided, to resort to the forces of Sir Charles Wilmot.

At that time Wilmot was in Kerry, laying waste the Desmond territories. Carew sent Captains Bostock and Barry out with a small force, to meet him and bring him back. Meanwhile, Carew reconnoitred the area that Tyrell was holding, and Tyrell in turn watched every movement that was made. He saw the small force heading north, but decided to reserve his ammunition for the more significant confrontation that would occur when they made their way back with Wilmot.

Donal was again absent, on this occasion because he was overseeing the situation at Dursey, and fearing that Ardea might come under attack Tyrell made the decision to take his horsemen over the mountains. Donnell MacCarthy and his men lent their support, and with over a thousand men under his command Tyrell began to harass and impede Wilmot and his forces. He attacked by night and also by day, when the army was on the march, and his tactics proved so successful that Wilmot welcomed Carew's orders to join him at Donemark.

Having first trailed his quarry, Tyrell then took his men ahead so that they could attack Wilmot as he marched through the narrow pass of Ceim an Fhia. The rebels were in position on the high rocks, ready to begin the assault, when a messenger arrived, and made a perilous approach to where Tyrell was overlooking his men. He brushed the messenger aside impatiently, whispering 'What is it, you fool? We are about to attack.'

'Forgive me, Captain' he replied as he struggled to catch his breath, 'But you should know that many sails have been sighted, to the west of Dursey.'

Tyrell swung around to look at the man. 'Spanish sails?'

'It's not clear, Captain.'

'Well they're not English are they? It must be the Spanish fleet at last!' Turning back to where his men were waiting he shouted 'Abandon the assault, the Spaniards have arrived! We will march to Glengarriff and await the good news from Donal Cam.'

So it was that Wilmot's forces, encountering no further obstacles to their path, made their way to Donemark. A number of companies were shipped across to Whiddy Island to join the troops who had already been camped there for over five weeks. More than a thousand soldiers were now assembled there, with five hundred more at Bantry Abbey, four hundred at Carriganass, and two thousand five hundred at Donemark. It was now a combined force that almost doubled those under Donal's command.

Captain Tyrell was back at the camp when he discovered that the sighted ships were not the long awaited Spanish fleet, but a convoy of some twenty English vessels on their way to the West Indies. He was beside himself with rage and humiliation, recognising that he had forfeited the opportunity of annihilating Wilmot's army and perhaps scuppering Carew's plans. Exhausted and dejected, he concluded that he was now fighting a losing battle. His brave and loyal men had suffered enough, and like himself were yearning for rest and for their homes. The time had come, he decided at last, to sue for peace.

The following morning, a section of the English army drew up on the south bank of the Coomhola River. As arranged, Tyrell and his men were on the north bank to meet them. Carew, however, was absent, and the Earl of Thomond there in his place.

Tyrell was suspicious, and shouted 'Where is Sir George?'

'My lord Carew has been taken ill' Thomond replied. 'I am here to represent him, and will convey your terms to him upon my return.'

There was no alternative but to comply, and so Tyrell began 'My lord, Donal Cam O'Sullivan, and His Majesty King Philip of Spain, send greetings to Her Majesty, and to her noble lords and loyal forces. They wish to offer their surrender to the Crown, on the following conditions: that you are to immediately cease all hostilities against King Philip, to whom all the lands of Donal O'Sullivan have been entrusted. You are to retire to the borders of those territories and await the envoy of His Majesty, who is at this time on his way from Spain to discuss a treaty. Finally, my men and I are to be guaranteed safe passage back to the territories of Hugh O'Neill. These are our terms.'

Thomond and his officers could scarcely believe what they were hearing; an Irish rebel leader dictating terms to them. There was some laughter, but the Earl himself was wise enough to say only 'Thank you, Captain Tyrell. I will go to Sir George with your message, and bring his response back to you as soon as possible.'

After more than five hours had elapsed, Tyrell began to suspect that there was some trickery afoot, and was on the verge of gathering his troops for departure when Thomond reappeared. 'Captain Tyrell' he shouted, 'Your terms have been rejected. Under the terms of the agreement reached with Don Juan de Aquila, who was acting for King Philip, Donal O'Sullivan is obliged to give Dunboy Castle up to us. My lord Carew further states that if your forces fail to surrender, no quarter will be given in any subsequent conflict.'

Tyrell almost snorted with laughter. 'I'll see you all in hell before I'll accept those terms. And if you ever reach Dunboy, it will be a long and bloody march for your army, which has already lost so many of its men.' Turning his back on the Earl, Tyrell fired three shots in the air as a signal to his troops to withdraw. It was the lack of communication and cooperation on Donal's part that angered Tyrell, even more than Carew's rebuff. Donal seemed to be riding out this storm in an ivory tower, concentrating on the hope of Spanish aid instead of the bloody battle taking place on the ground, and all that would be lost if they failed.

Tyrell was woken at sunrise with the news that a number of English ships had passed up the bay and entered Bantry before sunrise. Extricating himself quietly from his wife's arms, he dressed and then went out to rouse two messengers. One he sent to Dunboy, and the other to Ardea to inform Donal of his suspicion that Carew was about to transport his troops across the bay to Dunboy. Tyrell's intention was to attack the forces on Whiddy Island, and he asked Donal to send all his available small boats.

When the boats arrived at Ardnagashel in the darkness before the following dawn, Tyrell went over to Traclona beach on the northern side of Whiddy Island with four hundred of his best men and fifty horses. Breaking up into groups of about fifty, they approached the outer perimeter of the English camp without raising the alarm. As soon as all of his men were in position, Tyrell signalled them to attack.

The English forces were taken by surprise and thrown into panic, which increased when the rebels on horseback began to tear through the unprotected camp firing their weapons at will. Reenavanny Castle, which was poorly defended, was easily taken, and the battle was a short one. After a few hours the English troops abandoned their tents and supplies, and retreated to the shoreline carrying only their weapons. They were cornered now, and Tyrell's men picked them off effortlessly.

As the noise of the conflict reached the main camp, a mile across the harbour at Donemark, Carew was incredulous. He dispatched every boat in the harbour to go to the aid of his beleaguered force, and bring them back to the safety of the mainland. As they approached many of the soldiers were already backing into the water and swam out to the larger boats, while the smaller vessels came in to pick up the survivors left on the beach. Four to five hundred shot, drowned and fatally injured men were left behind, and retaliation promised to be severe. As the English ships began firing their cannons Tyrell gave the order to withdraw, and his forces made their way to the boats waiting on the north side of the island. With time at a premium, he was forced to leave the horses behind.

It had been a well-executed and satisfactory offensive, but as each day passed Tyrell grew more and more dissatisfied. His men were short of food now, he had lost so many opportunities of inflicting real damage on the English forces, and although there had been reports that Carew was in ill health he was an able tactician and a determined man. And while Donal Cam seemed to be avoiding any significant personal involvement, he was still the Commander in Chief and his orders must be obeyed. A visit, Richard decided, was in order.

Tyrell finally located Donal at Dunboy, and was further angered to find him relaxing in the great hall with his companions, apparently oblivious to what had been happening further up the bay. Without preamble he announced 'Since you are apparently content to sit back and wait for a Spanish fleet that will never arrive, I have told my men that we will be heading up north at first light tomorrow morning.'

A silence fell on the hall as Donal rose from his chair, never having expected that his captain would carry out this threat. 'You cannot leave, Richard. How will we go on without your aid?'

'Perhaps you could invite Carew to join you in your feasting, when he arrives at the gate.'

'To hell with Carew; the Spanish will be arriving at any moment and then all of our plans can be executed with ease.'

Tyrell laughed scornfully. 'If you still believe that the Spanish are coming then you are a fool. The English must know that they will never come now, or else they would be retreating to Cork. Why would Carew have sent those ships, without, support, if he didn't know that we stand alone?'

It was a question that Donal had so far ignored, and as the truth was forced upon him now he felt the foundations of all his hopes begin to crumble and fall.

Chapter Five

Carew's Army on the Move

After hours of heated discussion, Donal finally convinced Tyrell that he and Burke should remain at least until September, on the proviso that they would receive adequate food for their men. Donal undertook also to visit his captains at their camps and see for himself what further supplies were needed.

The Irish leaders might have been relieved to know that the situation in the enemy camp was deteriorating. During the second half of May the weather conditions were atrocious, featuring heavy rain and severe gales. It was so cold that a layer of snow came to rest on the tops of the higher hills, and fever was widespread at Donemark. Sick himself, Carew sat wrapped in blankets inside his tent, watching anxiously as his numbers slowly dwindled.

Suddenly, on the morning of the thirty-first, the weather brightened. Ignoring his own ill health Carew gave the order to march out to Kilavanoig, near Gearhies on the Muintir mBaire Peninsula. A number of companies were transported over to hold Whiddy Island, and then the ships departed the harbour. Only then did Carew himself move out, with the remaining section of his force.

On the following morning the English ships anchored close to the beach on the east side of League Point, and the Earl of Thomond and his men were the first to be ferried to the awaiting ships that would take them over to Berehaven. The armies of Sir Charles Wilmot and Sir Richard Percy followed later that day. Carew and his troops encamped at League Point that night, which was protected by the sea on three sides and a boggy marsh to the south. They joined their colleagues at Lawrence's Cove on Bere Island at about noon the next day, and set up camp on an eastern slope.

Tyrell had been observing this activity from the north shore of the bay, and sent word to Donal that the English army was approaching Dunboy by sea. Dividing his own force, he left Burke in command at Glengarriff while he headed for Dunboy with over four hundred horsemen. His spies had told him that Carew's force had been significantly weakened by disease and desertion, and it seemed likely that Donal could muster almost equal manpower, if not ordnance.

Donal Cam, meanwhile, was back at Ardea, where he was in talks with the Desmond chieftains. They had suffered at the hands of Wilmot and were now almost destitute, but willing to fight on nonetheless. Their meeting was interrupted by the arrival of a messenger from Dermod at Dursey, who brought the news that a Spanish ship had been sighted heading up Kenmare Bay. Donal threw up his arms in disbelief. Still, he told himself, maybe it was merely the advance guard, and his forces were in need of motivation. Immediately he sent riders out all over Beara with the news that the arrival of the Spanish fleet was imminent. Bonfires were lit all over the peninsula, and an air of celebration prevailed. Carew's landing was for the moment forgotten; salvation was at hand.

When the reports arrived at Dunboy Richard MacGeoghan, who was in charge of its defence, assumed that they now had the upper hand. Taking upon himself the role of mediator, he made the short sea journey across to Bere Island to parley with Carew and Thomond. Again, only the Earl appeared, and invited him into the main tent.

'I am here to talk of peace' MacGeoghan informed him. 'If we engage in battle then many lives will be lost unnecessarily. Dunboy is well fortified, and will not fall. The Spanish fleet is only hours away; the tide has turned in our favour.'

Thomond knew that only one ship had been sighted, and that their spies in Spain had not reported any potential aid for Ireland. He thought for a moment before answering 'I think you will find, Sir, that your information is wrong. No fleet has left Spain in the past month, and it would seem that your own position has been compromised. I would suggest therefore that you surrender Dunboy and so avoid, as you said, much unnecessary bloodshed.'

While Thomond and MacGeoghan were achieving this stalemate, Carew was aboard one of the English ships in the harbour surveying the Irish defences between Dunboy and Castledermot. He had hoped to make a landing, but found the whole area well fortified. At the last moment he noticed that the small island of Deenish, at the harbour's mouth, was deserted.

Within a few hours Carew was ashore, with two hundred and fifty troops and a few small falcon cannons. Detecting no movement of the Irish forces on the mainland he sent his troops across with orders to hold their position under the castle at Castledermot, at any cost. Another five hundred troops were then brought in to reinforce their position. On his way back from Bere Island MacGeoghan was horrified to see what Carew had achieved. With Tyrell and Burke east at Glengarriff and Donal over at Ardea, there was nobody in command of the line of defence here. Cursing their luck he urged his oarsmen to row faster so that he might get ashore to Dunboy, and raise the alarm.

Just as Carew's men were landing near Castledermot, the Spanish panache, Santiago, came into Kilmacalogue harbour. Before the anchor had been made fast Donal went aboard, where he was greeted by Captain Pedro Gonzales, Bishop Owen MacEgan and Donagh O'Driscoll, who had decided to return from Spain. The captain, who was first to speak, asked Donal if he still held Dunboy Castle for King Philip.

'I do' he replied, 'But without help we will lose it very soon. Where is the rest of the fleet?'

Bishop MacEgan wiped his brow with a cloth and then answered for Gonzales. 'Don't worry, Donal Cam, everything is in hand. King Philip has promised that another fleet will be sent here as soon as possible. I myself saw two thousand Spanish troops being mobilised.'

'But in God's name' cried Donal, 'When will they sail?'

'Soon, soon. And in the meantime we have for you enough money and enough arms and ammunition to hold out until they arrive.'

Donal sighed with relief. 'Thank God. I was beginning to lose hope.'

'Don't ever do that' the Bishop smiled. 'The Lord looks after his own in times of trouble. Now, if you will see that this letter reaches whoever is in charge at Dunboy, I will return to my cabin and pray for our swift deliverance.'

When the captain and Bishop MacEgan had left Donal turned to embrace Donagh O'Driscoll. 'It's good to see you again, Donagh. How are my boys?'

'They are thriving and happy at the Spanish court, Donal. I have a letter from them here.'

Tearing the letter open, Donal was dismayed to read that although they were being well treated in Spain, no aid was being organised at the present time. Don Juan de Aquila had misinformed his monarch, and convinced him not to send another fleet to Ireland. Looking up at Donagh with a wild expression, Donal demanded 'What is the meaning of this?'

'I'm sorry, Donal, but Bishop MacEgan lives in a dream. That bastard Aquila told King Philip that we were nothing but a pack of savages, and that despite his own heroic efforts at Kinsale we managed to incur defeat. The situation looks fairly hopeless now.'

After having his hopes raised yet again, Donal was devastated. Dunboy wouldn't hold out for more than a few weeks, and even if he sought aid from the O'Neills and O'Donnells it would take them longer than that to march south. Utterly dejected, he took the news back to his uncle Dermod at Ardea.

Dermod shared his nephew's sense of despair. 'What will you do now?'

'I don't know. I must think.' After a long silence, Donal went on 'If word gets out that the Spaniards have forsaken us we will be faced with a mass desertion. I think it best that we carry on as if they were still expected.'

'But the truth will come out, surely?'

'Not if we allow Bishop MacEgan to do all the talking. He could convince the devil himself that a fleet was already on its way up the bay. Now, if you will excuse me Uncle, I must go and get some rest.'

In the morning word came from Richard MacGeoghan that the English were on the mainland, and that he would hold out as long as he could, if possible until Michaelmas. Dermod went on ahead to Dunboy, while Donal returned to the Santiago, where he supervised the division of the money. When it was completed four boatloads of supplies, ammunition and arms, money and wine were brought ashore. As Donal prepared to depart he was joined by Father Dominic Collins, a Jesuit who had been a commander in the French army before he took religious orders. Donal was too downhearted to recognise it, but in Father Collins, Captain Tyrell and Captain Burke he had probably the best cavalry officers in the country. With over five hundred horsemen also at his disposal, he would have a significant advantage over the English side.

Tyrell had broken camp the previous day, and leaving his foot soldiers to follow on had gone ahead to Dunboy with one hundred and fifty mounted men. He arrived just as Carew's men were disembarking, and established a bridgehead just east of Castledermot Castle. Seeing the mass of English troops on Deenish Island, and the boats ferrying yet more across, he decided to split his small force in two. He would try and hold the mainland east of the stream with the defending force, which appeared to be leaderless. Then without warning the English were attacking Castledermot to his rear, and all he could do was dispatch eighty men to assist the forty or so trying to fight them off.

It was a heroic defence, but they were overpowered by cannon fire and sheer numbers, and abandoned the castle leaving forty men dead behind them. Tyrell watched as his men scrambled across the stream to safety. Looking around for his foot soldiers he shouted to William Burke 'Where are the rest of my men?'

'I don't know' Burke replied, 'I'll send a rider out to see what the delay might be.'

The English and their Irish allies advanced in waves across the small stream. Tyrell was obliged to order his men to fall back as they came under fire from the opposite bank. Entering the woods they regrouped, and succeeded in repelling any further English advance in that direction. They could not, however, prevent their spread westward along the shoreline, and eventual occupation of the little village.

Donal and Father Collins arrived with about twenty men as Tyrell was preparing to launch a counter attack. When they had dismounted, he asked angrily 'Where have you been? And what happened to the Spanish assistance you were so sure of?'

'They have been delayed. This is Father Collins. He is an experienced commander, and will organise the defence of Dunboy with MacGeoghan.'

'If you say so' said Tyrell dismissively. He knew that Donal was hiding the truth concerning the Spanish. 'Castledermot has been taken, and the English are established west along as far as Ceimatrenane. The rest of my men will be here shortly. Where are yours?'

'They are west at Eyeries and Ardea.'

'Are they? Sunning themselves while we get killed?'

Donal disliked Richard's constant sarcasm. 'My men will move when I tell them to' he said, sternly.

'Well then you had better tell them to, as we're about to lose everything.'

'I'll send for them now, Richard. You can take command of them while Dermod and I escort Ellen and some family members over to the safety of Dursey Castle. I'll be back by nightfall.'

By now almost speechless with rage, Tyrell shouted after Donal as he departed 'You may as well stay over there with the woman; only transfer command to me before you go!' He stared after his Commander in Chief, but Donal made no reply.

The boats were waiting at the landing area opposite Oilean Beag when the O'Sullivan family members and their servants arrived. Luckily the tide was changing, and they wouldn't have to deal with a fast current running through the channel. Donal embraced Ellen, who pleaded with him one last time to let her stay close by him.

'You must go, Ellen. You'll be safe at Dursey Castle, and I'll come for you as soon as I can.' The boatman shouted for the passengers to hurry, and Donal kissed Ellen's lips and held her close before nudging her gently towards the boat. He could not know then, that he would never see her again.

On his way back to Dunboy, Donal stopped at the family home near Eyeries. He was more than surprised to find his eldest son, Dermod, at the door of Kilcathrine Castle.

'Why are you not at Dunboy, Son?'

'I got word that mother was sick, and had to come and see her.'

Donal sighed. 'What ails her this time?'

'If you had been at her side, instead of with that other woman, you would know that she has been confined to her bed this last week.'

'It's not the first time. Now do you intend to join us?'

'I do not, Father. My mother and my sisters need me here.'

'As you wish, but I am sending them to Spain as soon as they can go. I will send a messenger if I consider you to be in danger.'

'You won't visit my mother?'

'I don't have the time, I must go.'

'You've had time for the other woman and her child, I suppose.'

'That is none of your business, Dermod. You have much to learn, my boy.'

'I am a man, Father, and I know that you have been bewitched by another man's wife, and that it will be the ruination of us all.'

Donal turned and mounted his horse, and rode away without bidding his son farewell.

Chapter Six

Surprise Attack

Lacking definitive orders from Donal regarding deployment, Tyrell decided to place his foot soldiers in a line, north of the English trenches. He planned to use the same tactics that had been so successful on Whiddy Island, but for this he needed the extra riders. Tyrell waited in vain for Donal's men to appear.

As Carew's forces continued to fortify their position, Tyrell and Burke led a number of attacks in an effort to prevent the advance on Dunboy. On each occasion they met with a barrage of musket shot from the well-drilled enemy force. Again, suing for peace began to look like the only viable option.

Two mornings later Tyrell entered the English camp west of the village under a white flag. On this occasion Carew himself was there to greet him, and the terms he offered proved to be extraordinary. 'Captain Tyrell' he began, 'I thank you for attending us here. I have heard many accounts of your bravery and skill in the field of battle, and would like to offer you the position of lieutenant over my own forces in Ireland.'

Trying not to betray his sense of shock, Tyrell enquired 'And my own forces? I suppose that my men will all hang for their part in our endeavours?'

Carew smiled warmly. 'Not at all, Captain. Any transgression will be forgotten and your men will remain under your command.'

Whatever Carew's intentions might have been, it seemed that they had produced the opposite effect, for Tyrell was suddenly reminded of the worthiness of his cause. Straightening himself in the saddle he replied 'My lord, your offer is extremely generous, but my leadership is not be bought by the highest bidder. We will fight on.'

Sir George was incredulous. 'But you came here to surrender! There is no help arriving from Spain, your cause is lost!'

'It is far from lost. Remember how many men you have already lost. We have a force to almost match your own, and God on our side.'

'This fine talk, Captain, but you have already been warned that you will be given no quarter if hostilities resume.'

'And I give you the same warning. If I dispose of your boats you will be without means of escape. I would suggest that you leave now.'

Carew clapped his hands. 'Bravo! I definitely should have you under my command.' He offered his hand to Tyrell, who took it briefly before wheeling his horse around.

'Farewell, Sir George' he shouted into the wind.

'You're a fool, Richard' William Burke muttered when they had returned to camp. 'Carew was offering us surrender without shame.'

'Does it mean nothing to you, what we're fighting for? And do you really trust that snake?'

'It doesn't matter what I think. We have already lost if Donal Cam and his men are not at our side. We are mere scapegoats here, and I can see nothing but death before us. We must head back north while we still can.'

'We'll give it a week, William, no more I promise you.'

By nightfall there was still no sign of Donal or his army. Tyrell was too restless to sleep, and summoning four men he rode to Dunboy. Approaching from the west, he avoided the English positions and rode straight up to the main gates. Finding no guards there, or sentries on the walls, he fired a warning shot and then waited. After a few minutes a man appeared, swaying slightly, on the wall. 'Friend or foe' he shouted, 'Who is there?'

'Get off the wall you drunken fool, open the bloody gates and go and tell MacGeoghan that Captain Tyrell is here.'

At that point another man appeared on the wall demanding to know who was there, and Tyrell grew so exasperated that he took a pot shot at the wavering figure. He made sure that the shot missed, but panic filled the air. The warning bell on the tower was ringing, and inside the castle men leapt from their beds fearing an English attack. As he approached the doors Tyrell had to bellow for admittance until he was recognised, and finally allowed to take his men into the bawn where MacGeoghan was waiting for him. 'Captain Tyrell . . .' he began

'What in God's name is going on here? Where's Collins, and who was on guard?'

'Father Collins was called away. But I had six men on the walls by the gate' MacGeoghan replied.

'No you did not.'

'I will find out who was responsible, Richard, and remedy the situation.'

'You can dismiss your so-called sentries; I'll bring in forty of my best men before dawn. Let the Spaniards stay though, they can man the cannons.'

'But Donal picked these men himself.'

'To hell with Donal O'Sullivan; if he gave a damn about Dunboy he'd be here now.'

Over in the English camp a council of war was in progress following the arrival of the White Knight Lord Barry, John Barry, Cormac MacDermot, and Owen O'Sullivan. They had come over land without encountering any rebel forces, and had with them over six hundred men including two hundred on horseback. Sir Owen, who had resided at Dunboy for a number of years, was able to give a very accurate description of its buildings and of its present defences. After only a few hours, a plan of attack had been formed. When a spy came in from Dunboy, Owen was the first to question him. 'Do you know whether my wife remains in the castle?'

'I think, not, my lord. The only women there are cooking for the men or helping with the reinforcements. I have heard a rumour that Donal took her west to Oilean Beag a few days ago.'

Sir Owen turned away with a bitter expression on his face. 'Well he won't be keeping her there, God damn him.'

When Donal arrived at Ardea to gather his troops and lead them back over the mountains, he discovered that Philip, his favourite uncle, had died suddenly a few hours earlier. He had seemed in the best of health, and was planning to sail to Spain and petition the king himself, and this was a sad blow for Donal both politically and personally. While his uncle Dermod made hasty burial arrangements Donal went aboard the Santiago to give the captain a number of letters. Gonzales was waiting only for a favourable wind before returning to Spain. In his letter to King Philip Donal had not only urged him to send help, but outlined in full the true circumstances of Don Juan de Aquila's surrender. If aid was not forthcoming, he concluded, then ships should be sent to take himself, his family and followers back to Spain.

That evening, while Donal was at Ardea and Tyrell was preparing for a more concentrated attack on the newly placed gun positions, Carew received information that a strong force with three cannons had been dispatched to Oilean Beag. Aware now that his wife was there, Owen O'Sullivan immediately offered to take a force over land.

'And how will your men reach the island' Carew enquired, 'Swim across?'

Embarrassed by his rash suggestion, Sir Owen made no reply.

'You can take five boats and a hundred and fifty men, with Captains Bostock and Fleming, and Lieutenant Downing. And leave this night, under cover of darkness.'

The ships arrived offshore at dawn, taking everyone by surprise. A messenger was dispatched to Ardea to request Donal's help, but when he arrived a requiem mass was in progress and he was not permitted to interrupt it. Unwilling to pass his information on, he had no option but to wait until the mass was over. As the funeral cortege headed towards the family graveyard the messenger tried to approach Donal but was brushed aside.

'Get away from me you madman' Donal growled. 'Can't you see I am burying my uncle?'

'Forgive me, my lord, but the English are attacking Dursey Castle.'

'Why would they do that, you fool? Get out of my way.'

The exasperated messenger rode away, cursing Donal Cam under his breath, but Dermod had heard the exchange and asked if they shouldn't investigate the claim.

'All in good time, Son' was all that his distraught father replied; 'Let us first bury our dead.'

Aboard the Merlin, Captain Bostock was searching for a way ashore at Dursey Island, which stood across from Oilean Beag and gave the castle its name; when he had located the landing place he ordered Lieutenant Downing to take a company of soldiers and a few falcons on to the island. As they approached, the islanders grabbed what belongings they could and charged across the bridge to the safety of the castle on Oilean Beag. Downing established a base at the ruins of the church of St Michael the Archangel, which had been almost destroyed by pirates some years earlier. The castle stood below them across a narrow gulley to the southeast, well within range.

When Fleming and O'Sullivan had made their way on to Oilean Beg and towards the castle ramparts, Captain Bostock ordered all the cannons on board the Merlin to open fire. It was the signal for Downing's men to commence firing also, and for the others to mount their attack on the walls and ramparts.

There was great consternation within. Conor O'Driscoll found that they had brought the wrong ammunition for the cannons, and in addition most of the powder was damp after its crossing. Unable to return fire, he marshalled all of his men on the east side of the castle and attempted to defend it with the small arms available. It was a lost cause, and he knew it.

After about four hours of cannon fire from land and sea, a frontal attack on the walls and ramparts was mounted and Conor O'Driscoll ordered his men to surrender. The white flag was raised, and the cannon fire ceased. Recognising Owen O'Sullivan at the head of the troops, O'Driscoll sent one of his men to hide Ellen in the castle cellar. He and two others ran along the western wall and escaped down a cave spout, to a ledge at the water's edge where they prayed they would not be discovered.

When Captain Bostock arrived to find O'Driscoll gone, he ordered that every one of the remaining rebels be lined up against a wall and shot, regardless of their sex. Owen O'Sullivan rushed in with a number of men and searched the castle until he located his wife hiding in the cellar with some other women. Catching her by the hair he dragged her up the stairway, leaving his soldiers behind to assault the rest of the women in any way that they chose. When they reached the open air he swung Ellen round to face him, asking 'Where is your beloved Donal Cam now? Who is going to save you from a good whipping, you little whore?'

'Say what you like' Ellen spat at him, 'But I'll never play your wife now.'

'You have disgraced my name, but you are my wife and I will never let you out of my sight again. You'll be confined to a small chamber at Carriganass until the day that you die.'

Satisfied that the job was complete, Captain Bostock ordered that the castle be blown up. In case of any attempt to retake the island, he left a garrison of forty men behind. The English ships, now carrying Sir Owen's wife as well as the arms and supplies that had been gathered, sailed away from Oilean Beag.

At Ardea Castle, the feasting following the burial was underway when a rider came in from the west shouting for Donal Cam. 'What is it' asked Donal as he emerged from a group of men with a wine goblet in his hand.

'I come from Captain Tyrell. The English attacked Dursey Castle this morning. The castle was taken and everyone killed.'

A shocked silence was broken by Donal's cry: 'That is not

possible! Was Conor O'Driscoll not there to defend it?' What happened to my Ellen?'

'I'm sorry, my lord, but that is all I know. Captain Tyrell said to tell you that Dunboy will also fall, if your army does not arrive immediately.'

Donal looked up at his uncle Dermod in bewilderment. 'This cannot be true; surely fate would not be so cruel, as to take away two people so dear to me within a few days?'

'All is not lost yet, Donal. We must get the rest of the family members on board the Santiago, for she will sail at any time. Then we will see what your army is made of. Now on to your feet, there is work to be done.'

After a sleepless night Donal rose very early the following morning, and climbing up to the battlements he watched the Santiago unfold her sails and catch the cool dawn breeze at the beginning of her long voyage. The previous night he had seen family and friends safely aboard. His thoughts, though, were with Ellen. He wanted to go to Dursey and search for her himself, and yet he knew he would not be able to bear it if he discovered her dead in the ruins.

The shout of 'Rider in from the west' brought Donal to his senses, and down to the bawn where Conor O'Driscoll was dismounting. 'What happened, Conor' he pleaded, 'Where is Ellen?'

'We were taken by surprise at dawn; myself and two men managed to escape but the rest were killed. Ellen, I think, was taken away by your cousin.'

'Oh thank God; at least she will still be alive. And how did you escape?'

'We went over the cliff face, and hid in that western cave until the ships had departed. A small boat from Ballycrovane picked us off the rocks before the tide came in.'

'My uncle will need to know which of his friends and neighbours were lost. You can go to him in his chamber, Conor, thank you.' Donal knew that Dermod would have much grieving to do.

As for himself, he went to find his infant son. Here, at least, was a part of his beloved Ellen; they would comfort each other in the dark days of her absence.

As Tyrell waited by Dunboy, he was at a loss as to his next action. His rider had returned from Ardea without any orders from the grief-stricken Donal, and time was surely running out. He decided at last that he should make one last attack on the strongest and most westerly of the English camps, where Carew himself was based. If he could overpower the troops there, it was just possible that Carew might think again about Dunboy.

He mounted the attack two hours before dawn, with some three hundred horsemen. He had expected everyone to be asleep, but to his distress he found the English forces up and alert. His plan had somehow been betrayed. After a few rounds of concentrated fire he was forced to withdraw, with over fifty of his best men dead or wounded.

When they had returned to camp, Tyrell called Burke aside. 'We have spies among our ranks, William, and we must find out who they are.'

'Four new men have joined us during this last week. It's possible that one or more of them are followers of Owen O'Sullivan I suppose.'

'Then we'll put them to the test. Spread the word that we plan to retake Castledermot and cut off the English retreat.'

As Tyrell and Burke watched the enemy lines, they eventually noted an obvious movement of troops eastwards. The erroneous information had certainly reached the English officers. Shortly afterwards two of the new men rode back into camp. They pleaded their innocence at first, and then offered to deliver more false information; but Tyrell ignored their protestations, and the two of them were shot.

Exhausted and demoralised, Tyrell lay down to sleep for a while. Almost immediately he was woken by the sound of cannon fire. He sprinted up to the high ground overlooking the English camp, but could see nothing. When the firing began again, he looked around until he realised, with mounting horror, that the puffs of gun smoke were coming from the west and the north of Dunboy Castle. Through his eyeglass he could see that considerable damage had already been done to the tower house itself.

Charging back through the camp, Tyrell shouted for his men to reform. As they marched quickly along the narrow neck of land they were met by a barrage of musket shot from two lines of soldiers. 'Fall back' he shouted angrily. 'There is nothing we can do.'

Chapter Seven

The Fall of Dunboy

As the bombardment continued on that morning in June, 1602, Tyrell and Burke were all too aware that another attack on the well-entrenched English forces would be suicidal, and that without the assistance of Donal's army they were helpless. Why had he not at least come over the mountains and raised a siege? The delay was inexplicable, and messengers sent to solicit his aid came back as mystified as they left. Tyrell mounted a few skirmishes against the gun emplacement to the west of the castle, but failed to even dent the strong supporting force.

The gun batteries continued to fire throughout the afternoon of the sixteenth, and soon the top part of the tower house had been partially destroyed as well as a portion of the western fortification. Realising that it was only a matter of time until Dunboy was in ruins, Father Collins sent a man in, under a white flag, to inform the enemy that he was willing to discuss surrender. The man had walked only twenty yards when he was shot in the head.

By the evening of that day the continuous pounding had created an opening in the outer wall by the northwest corner. The first wave of English troops assaulted the breach, and after hand-to-hand battle the sheer number of their opponents forced the castle's defenders to retreat. They sought refuge in the eastern section, as the troops occupied the bawn. While MacGeoghan was ordering his men to the tower, Father Collins was giving the conflicting order that every man should save himself. Confused, about forty of them tried to escape over the western bawn wall but were met by a barrage of musket fire. Observing the fate of their colleagues some of the others tried to swim for safety but were shot, or pierced by the spears of the soldiers waiting in the longboats. Fearful for his own life, Father Collins surrendered and was quickly taken prisoner.

As the sun rose on the morning of the seventeenth, Tyrell and Burke were resigned to their defeat. They had already lost half of their men, and would not risk more. Tyrell's main concern now was his remaining force of about eighty men, and the other men and women who were still inside the castle. Donal Cam, he reflected, clearly placed no value on their lives.

Despite the increasingly desperate messages from his officers and the exhortations of his uncle Dermod, Donal flatly refused to leave Ardea. He was convinced that he should keep his army intact until such time as the Spanish fleet arrived, even if Dunboy must be sacrificed. With such a strong combined force, he believed, he could then drive the English back to Cork, and possibly out of Ireland altogether. The armies of the north would join him, and the English would be forced at last to relinquish their domination of the country. He would then, of course, be hailed the great liberator of Ireland.

While Donal was praying with Father Archer for the fulfilment of this destiny, word arrived that Ellen had escaped her guards and thrown herself from the tower house at Carriganass. The river outside was fast flowing and her body had not been found. Donal was utterly desolate, devastated and furious. 'Why' he demanded of father Archer 'Why did God allow this? Am I to be punished continuously for my love of another man's wife?'

'We must learn to accept God's will' the priest replied. 'Let us pray for Ellen's soul.'

'No! I have confessed my sins, I have flayed myself and begged to be pardoned, and it is never enough! What more does He want?'

'I cannot answer that, Donal. But you must not give up hope.'

'Hope of what? My castle is being destroyed, my family scattered to the four winds; I wait here for aid that will never come, while our country is given over to foreigners, and now my darling Ellen is gone from me too. Your precious bloody God has forsaken me, and there is nothing left to hope for.'

'Stop' cried Father Archer, 'It is sinful to speak this way, as if you mean to make recourse to the devil!'

'Get out' Donal roared as he threw a bag of coins across the floor, 'Your damned church has never been of any use to me! Get out and take your forty pieces of silver with you.'

Servants and soldiers scattered as Donal emerged, ranting still and throwing aside anything in his path, from the oratory. As he descended the steps towards a hidden chamber near the dungeon he was shouting 'I come to release you, brother'; several members of his retinue decided to leave the castle altogether.

There were many stories and legends regarding the hidden room in the depths of Ardea, which was supposed to have been haunted ever since the castle was built. Some said that a madman was incarcerated there, while others believed that it had been built for the devil himself. These stories would have carried less weight if there had not been several reports over the years of unearthly sounds coming from the chamber. Only two servants know the true identity of its occupant, and they had been sworn to secrecy upon pain of death.

That night was a terrifying one for those who stayed at Ardea. Even the women looking after Donal and Ellen's infant lost their nerve, and shortly before midnight they gathered the boy up in blankets and fled. The strange sounds of shaken chains, roaring and howling, shouts of laughter and maniacal screaming rose through the castle and reverberated throughout that black night. As dawn approached a silence fell at last, and then Donal appeared. He was climbing the stairs to the main hall, with what appeared to be another human struggling along beside him. The creature had wild, matted hair on his head and his face, and was covered in dirt. His feet were clubbed, and resembled something closer to hooves.

The secret of Donal's twin had been well kept. Born with serious physical deformities he had been locked up, out of sight, for his own benefit. He could be reasonable and lucid, but his great anger lent him a surprising strength. Only in Donal's presence was he consistently calm. The servants who brought him food every day had insisted that he be chained up, suspecting that he was capable of killing the two of them with ease. Donal called these servants to him now, and with his help they washed and dressed his brother in new clothes, cut his hair and trimmed his beard, so that he appeared almost normal.

MacGeoghan and his remaining men were still holding the lower part of the tower house with the aid of Thomas Taylor, a brother in law of Captain Tyrell's. After another bout of continuous cannon fire another English assault was mounted, and direct combat recommenced. As darkness fell the defending force was pushed back, down into the large cellars under the great hall where the gunpowder had been stored.

Urged forward by their officers the English continued their advance down the winding stairs, and soon gained entrance to the cellars. MacGeoghan was himself injured, and aware that no mercy would be shown he was attempting to ignite the great kegs of gunpowder, when he was shot dead. Those remaining alive, fifty-eight in total including five women, had no alternative but to surrender. They were confined in the bawn overnight, and then taken to the English camp at daybreak while Carew's instructions were awaited.

With victory achieved, Sir George was in no hurry to deal with his prisoners. His priority, shrewdly enough, was to reward the loyalty of his men and his Irish allies. A great celebration began, at which all the food and drink that had been removed from Dunboy was be consumed, and it continued well into the following day, and night.

Tyrell and Burke were distraught; they had known in the end

that Dunboy would fall, but it should have been able to hold out for months, not days. Their feelings towards Donal had reached a level that went beyond disappointment or anger, and with no communication from him now they sent a messenger to Carew, requesting a meeting to discuss an honourable pardon.

Carew's reception, as they might have expected, was less cordial than it had been before. His officers treated them with an unnerving callousness, and Sir George himself came into their presence half dressed and almost oblivious of their presence. Buttoning his uniform slowly, he fixed Captain Tyrell with a glare and asked what it was that he wanted.

'The release of my twelve remaining men, Sir, who surrendered and are being held by you.'

Carew ordered his guard to go and fetch all of Tyrell's followers with the exception of his brother-in-law, Thomas Taylor. They were lined up along the beach, with an escort of armed redcoats.

'And what do you have to trade for their lives?'

'If you release them into my hands I give you my word that I will leave Beara; if you guarantee a safe passage, I will return with my followers to the northern territories.'

'Do you not realise, Captain Tyrell, that your fight is over, and has come to nothing as I warned you that it would? Where is your great leader, anyway? You can only save yourself and your men by availing of my offer, and joining my forces.'

'Thank you, sir, but I cannot in conscience accept.'

'And that is your final answer?'

'It is, your lordship.'

'So be it' Carew replied. He raised his hand and the redcoats lifted their muskets and aimed; the hand dropped, and as sudden gunfire tore through the morning air the prisoners fell lifeless to the ground.

Tyrell cried out 'God Almighty, there was no need for that! They had families at home, every one of them!'

'You had your chance' Sir George said quietly. 'Now take your leave, Captain, before I shoot you myself.'

Following Tyrell and Burke's retreat over the mountains, Carew ordered that the remaining prisoners were to be marched into Castletown's village square, where they were summarily executed in full view of the local population. Eight hundred troops were then dispatched with instructions to find, and kill, anyone who might have been connected with the rebels. Animals were also slaughtered, crops and dwellings destroyed. The main core of the English army was meanwhile being transported over to Bere Island, and then back up the bay to the beach near League Point where they had originally disembarked some weeks earlier. Carew's own gunnery officers were sent to blow up what remained of Dunboy, so that not even a stone remained upon a stone.

More than satisfied with the outcome of his campaign, Carew departed on the twenty-fourth of June with the remaining section of his army, landing at Whiddy Island that evening. After spending the night at Reenavanny Castle he crossed to the mainland at Donemark while Reenavanny was levelled behind him, to ensure that it was of no further use to the O'Sullivans.

When his entire army was assembled at Donemark, Carew ordered a head count. He was concerned to find that it had been something of a Pyrrhic victory; over two thousand men –half of his original force— were dead or missing. It had, nonetheless, been a conclusive victory, and there was little chance of an attempted Spanish invasion now. As for Donal O'Sullivan, who had begun so well and whose officers had fought with such determination, Sir George was as mystified by his absence as everyone else.

Early on the morning of the twenty-sixth the order was given to break camp, and the soldiers moved off towards Cork. The Earl of Thomond boarded the Merlin and set sail for England, to inform the Queen that the insurrection in the southwest of Ireland had been quelled. Carew sailed to Cork aboard the Trinity, taking the prisoners Thomas Taylor, and Father Collins with him. On arrival, Tyrell's brother-in-law was strung up in chains at the North Gate Bridge, while the Jesuit was taken to Youghal, which was his birthplace, and hanged by the main gates.

When Tyrell and Burke thought it safe to ride out once more they returned to Dunboy to survey the damage. Almost nothing was left of the castle, and the smell of rotting corpses hung heavily in the air. Even in the village there was not a soul to be seen, and the ground was strewn with the bodies of humans and animals alike. Coming across a pack of dogs eating the remains of a child, Burke started to retch. He discharged his rifle to scatter them, bringing Tyrell to his side. Despondently, he asked 'What are we going to do now?'

'To be honest, William, I'm not sure.'

'Ah Richard, the men have had enough and so have I. The few that are left want to return to their families, and I can't say that I blame them.'

'It's true that the place reeks of death. We'll head east to Glengarriff and make camp there tonight, where at least we still have some supplies. We can decide what to do once we're there.'

'Well then I think I'll take a few men and ride over to Ardea and find out for myself what Donal Cam's explanation might be. Will you come?'

'I'll have nothing more to do with that man' Tyrell replied darkly. 'He may still be Commander in Chief, but as far as I'm concerned he's a disgrace to the Irish nation.'

As he crossed the pass north of Adrigole, Burke could see smoke rising in the distance. Donal's army had been so close, and yet they might as well have been on the moon. His blood boiled when he thought of all the men, and women too, who had laid down their lives while Donal sat nursing his grievances at Ardea.

Donal's soldiers stared at Burke and his men as they rode through the camp, their clothes and their horses dirty and bedraggled. William's strained emotions snapped and he roared 'What in the hell are you lazy bastards staring at? We've been fighting your battles over the hill, damn you all!'

One of the older men stepped forward. 'We are not lazy, Captain, and many of us have died from the fever here that would have preferred to die in battle. It is not courage that we lack, only a leader. All we want now is to be allowed to march home.'

'I am on my way to talk to Donal O'Sullivan' said Burke, relenting. 'Head for the woods of Glengarriff, and I will see you there.'

The crowd of people at the outer gates of the castle told Captain Burke that something was amiss. Dismounting, he approached a group of local men and asked them what was happening.

'Donal Cam has thrown Father Archer out and released some kind of devil from the dungeons. Bishop MacEgan and some other priests are inside there now, trying to exorcise it.'

'What rameshing is this?' Burke was surprised by such talk, but he had forgotten where he was; the old pagan beliefs were as strong as ever down here in Beara.

'It is the truth I tell you! If you had heard about what went on in there last night, you would be down on your knees praying.'

Burke led his men away, until word came out that the exorcism had been completed, and that the strange beast inside had taken on a human form once more. All those who had business inside were then free to enter the castle walls, where they heard that a feast would be held in honour of Bishop MacEgan. Burke and his men lingered in the grounds for a while, talking with a group of soldiers who were drinking in a corner of the bawn. They were clearly still terrified, but Burke decided to make his entrance.

The great hall was full of people now, but at first William was unable to see Donal anywhere. At last he spotted him, sitting at the end of the table talking to a stranger in a long black cloak. As he approached the two men, something made him look at the floor; the stranger wore no boots, and instead of feet he appeared to have some kind of hooves. Panicking, Burke started to turn back but Donal saw him, and beckoned him closer. The stranger turned around and Burke shivered, for the eyes that met his own were the eyes of an animal, and then the animal bared his teeth, and growled. He must have lost his mind altogether, William thought as he ran back through the crowd of people, none of whom seemed to have noticed this cursed beast in the corner. Sweating and shaking he leapt up onto his horse and rode for the mountain, all the time feeling those eyes, those teeth, those hooves at his back.

Chapter Eight

Another Spanish Ship

Tyrell had already established the camp in Glengarriff woods when Burke arrived. Both he and his horse were bathed in sweat, and even before he had dismounted he was asking for something to drink. Tyrell passed him a jug of poteen, asking 'What in the name of God is wrong with you? What happened?'

'You wouldn't believe it if I told you' Burke replied, gasping for breath.

'Tell me, William!'

'Well . . . they told me that Donal had released some kind of a demon from the dungeons, and when I went in he was there in the hall, talking with Donal . . .'

'The demon was talking to Donal? Have you lost all reason, man?'

'I'm telling you he was there; didn't I see his clubbed feet myself?'

Tyrell shook his head, wondering if the recent defeat had unbalanced his friend's mind. 'Come into the tent, William. I don't want the men hearing this story of yours.'

The two men talked for a long time, until Tyrell accepted that there must have been some truth in Burke's account of events; he seemed quite sane after all. Whatever the truth of it, Donal was obviously not to be relied upon at present; their predicament was clearly unchanged.

Sir Charles Wilmot was the last officer to move his troops - he still had eight hundred and about sixty horses - out of Donemark. Tyrell and Burke watched from the high cliffs near the pass as the column marched out through the Borlin Valley into Kerry. It was obvious that Wilmot was returning to Desmond to complete the task of breaking up the remaining rebel forces, but they were powerless to intervene. Wilmot's men were the best trained in the English forces, and they themselves had little shot or gunpowder left.

When word arrived at Ardea that a Spanish ship had been sighted, Donal was cautiously excited. It might have been sent to collect them, or it might be that military aid was finally on its way. Although the hour was late, at least his own actions would be justified at last. Taking himself to the battlements he began his vigil, searching the sky beyond the western headland for Spanish sails and praying. Dermod joined him there, and looked out at the horizon sadly. 'It is too late, Donal. They may as well have waited until we were all dead.'

Donal looked up at him. 'What if it is the ship that will carry us all to Spain? We will all be dead if we stay here.'

'You want to leave the rest of them behind to face the consequences? You are still the Commander in Chief, Donal; you can't mean it?'

'What is there to stay for, Uncle? Only more bloodshed.'

Dermod turned away angrily, saying 'You go if you must; I would die before I'd abandon my loyal men and run.'

The Spanish panache made the harbour entrance, her sails flapping in the evening breeze, just as the sun was setting over the mountain. Donal recognised the Santiago, and was anxious to hear what news she brought. A number of the allied chieftains had also heard of her arrival, and were on their way.

On board the Santiago Captain Gonzales greeted Donal, and assured him that his sons were well before breaking the bad news that he had been expecting. 'There are no other ships, Donal, I'm sorry. We are alone.'

'Bishop MacEgan told me that the fleet was being prepared.'

'It was discussed, señor, but the King decided against it at the last moment. Word reached him that Dunboy had fallen, and you were defeated.'

'But we still have an army of almost two thousand men intact; I was waiting only for the arrival of the King's men.'

'I'm sorry, but my orders are to collect you, and any of your friends or family that wish to return to Spain. I am not to delay.'

Donal said nothing, but called for his boatman to take him ashore.

A meeting of all the allies was called, and went on for several hours. After lengthy argument and discussion, Donal and Dermod declared that they would fight on, but the others felt that the fight was lost. Many of them decided to avail of the opportunity of escape to Spain. They included the O'Driscoll brothers, two of the O'Mahony clan, Father Archer, his own son Dermod and sister Orla. They were to sail on the seventh of July, and Orla pleaded with her brother to allow her to take his infant son with her to safety. Donal declined on the grounds that he was too fragile to survive the voyage, and would later be glad that he did. Tragedy was to strike his family once more that year; twenty-four hours after the ships departure from Kenmare Bay, his beloved sister was lost overboard.

Over the next few months Donal was loathe to move out of his stronghold in Ardea. The public and personal misfortunes of recent times had taken their toll, and he was without plans or hopes. Wilmot was rampaging through Desmond, forcing the people out of their homes and into west Limerick so that any aid or assistance would be beyond Donal's reach. Clan leaders were evicted from their castles, and some of them left destitute, begging for food on the roadside.

On this occasion, as before, it was Dermod who managed to rouse Donal from his torpor. Striding into his chamber one day he demanded 'How can you sit here and do nothing while

Wilmot is laying waste Desmond? I may be an old man, but by God if you won't lead our forces out then I will, if I die in the attempt.'

He left his nephew alone then, and that evening Donal ate with his uncle. 'I will take my forces out, Dermod' he said quietly. 'I hope that you will stay to look after the castle, and those here that have entrusted their lives to me.'

The remaining force numbered only about five hundred, as many had deserted or had fallen ill. They set off two days later eastwards along the Nedeen River into west Muskerry, and then into the O'Donovan territory. The clan had joined Carew's forces in the destruction of Dunboy and Donal exacted his revenge now, burning crops and barns, and turning livestock loose. His scouts brought him the news that Captain Harvey was employing a policy of 'torched earth' along the coast of West Cork, and taking all the O'Mahony and MacCarthy castles. As they moved west towards Leamcon Castle, Donal began to harass Harvey's army, attacking at night and skirmishing during the day. At the same time, Bishop MacEgan had gathered a sizeable force, including even some of the MacCarthys who had sided with the Crown. Feeling betrayed by the Bishop regarding the Spanish situation, Donal made the decision not to join their forces together, and he was to regret it. His own men were outnumbered and forced to retreat westward, and another valuable opportunity was lost.

Captain Tyrell, meanwhile, had moved his camp close to Inchigeela in Muskerry. He was trying to feed his men by raiding as far as the Lee Valley. An additional fifty men had managed to journey south to join his force, but his wife was still with him and he was now seriously considering returning home. Her brother had almost persuaded him to do so, when one morning a guard alerted him to the approach of a group of horsemen. Putting his men on standby he went to see for himself, and was amazed to find Donal riding in. 'I never thought to see you again.'

'I know, Richard, but I had my reasons. I am here now.'

'Come into the tent, Donal, I will send someone for food and drink.'

After Donal Cam's humble entrance, Tyrell offered no further recriminations. The past was past, his commander had suffered greatly, and they must look to the future now. Finally, they agreed that they would work together for another two months, and cover themselves by petitioning both the Spanish King for further aid, and the English Queen for peace.

When Donal's letter reached Queen Elizabeth she was not amused. Well she remembered the references to herself in his intercepted letter to King Philip. "A bald buzzard hawk" he had called her, and a "Dry old hag whom God will surely turn to stone". She called her court advisers to her side, and ultimately decided to react by dispatching an additional one thousand troops to Munster, to annihilate Donal and his allies once and for all. The O'Neills and O'Donnells had been subdued, and he was the last remaining thorn in her side.

Donal's situation was looking grim until Cormac MacDermot of Muskerry escaped from prison and decided to join the rebels. Regaining Macroom Castle, where he had been held, he summoned all of his forces together and sent for Donal and his officers.

Leaving their forces encamped about three miles to the west of Macroom, Donal Cam, Tyrell and Burke made their way to the castle, having been invited to stay there for a few days. When MacDermot's followers learned of his plans, they arrived en masse to voice their objections. They had suffered the loss of cattle and foodstuffs during the previous months, and felt that they would be incapable of sustaining such a large army now, with winter approaching. MacDermot, however, came out to assure them that as soon as he was ready the men would be heading into West Cork to engage the English there. As he turned to go back inside, a messenger arrived from Carew.

MacDermot's two sons had also been imprisoned, one in the Tower of London and another at Blarney Castle, and Carew was warning him that they would "surely suffer the consequences of any rash action on his part". Showing the letter to Donal, he asked him 'What will I do? They could execute both of my sons if I go into open rebellion.'

Donal thought for a moment before answering. 'I think you should send a letter back telling Carew that you have been in ill health since your imprisonment, and have no intention of revolting from your sick bed. It should satisfy him, until our plans are made.'

Cormac had no sooner sat down to write the letter than another messenger arrived, with the news that a Sir Charles Bagnall had arrived in Cork with a thousand troops, and was already at Inniscara on the way to Macroom. They were all shaken by this information, and aware that their hand was now being forced. MacDermot felt that he simply couldn't gamble with the lives of his sons. 'I'm very sorry' he said to Donal that evening, 'But I've decided to tell Carew that I remain a servant of the Crown. I don't have any option.'

Donal was crestfallen, but sympathetic. 'I would probably do the same, Cormac. We will move out so that your position is not compromised. If the situation changes we will talk again.'

That same night Donal departed for Ardea with two hundred men, Burke set off on a foraging expedition with twenty, while Tyrell returned to the original camp near Inchigeela with the remaining thousand or so. Bagnall came into Muskerry, and went immediately to visit Cormac MacDermot. There seemed to be no doubt in Cormac's mind now, as to where his allegiances lay. Whilst he was entertaining Bagnall at Macroom Castle, he sent two of his relations into Tyrell's camp with some useless information, and they returned with a complete picture of the layout of the camp. It was quickly passed on to Bagnall, and with MacDermot's assistance he launched an attack the following night. Tyrell and his men were caught completely off guard, and would have been wiped out were it not for the accidental discharge of a musket affording them a few moments warning.

The alarm was raised as the English forces were already breaking through the outer defences, and there was mayhem throughout the camp. Tyrell shouted for his men to flee to the woods in the darkness and he and his wife followed suit, dressed as they were in their nightshirts and leaving all their belongings behind. All of their cattle and horses had to be abandoned, their arms and ammunition, countless items of lace, silk and velvet, and a casket of Spanish gold.

As they trudged westward in heavy rain and strong winds, Tyrell recognised that it could have been worse; at least he and his wife had survived, and he had lost only a dozen men. That traitor Cormac, though, he cursed, swearing that he would avenge the betrayal. With his wife Aoife mounted on their solitary horse, he led his half-clothed, unarmed and hungry band of men over the mountains on foot. Marching day and night, they arrived ay Ardea the following evening.

As soon as he saw them, Donal rode out to meet Tyrell with extra horses. Over a good meal and plenty of wine he heard the story of their betrayal, noting that MacDermot was a weak and immoral man. When Burke arrived at the castle and heard the news he wanted to head back to Muskerry immediately, to exact vengeance on the traitor. The men, however, needed to eat properly and rest for a while, and so they set out three mornings later on the twenty-first of October. Tyrell, Burke, three hundred men and fifty horses entered Muskerry without regard for the news that Bagnall was still in the area, and that Captain Flower was stationed east by Crowley's Castle with four hundred men.

Dividing their forces they began raiding by night, and laying waste the territories of Cormac's treacherous relations the MacSweeney's and MacTeig MacCarthy. They plundered and then burned their homes and their crops, and reclaimed the cattle that had been stolen from Tyrell's camp. There was no sign of the Spanish gold. When Bagnall and Flower began to close in they rejoined and made for Glengarriff, driving the cattle before them. They had enough food to last them well into the winter now.

By mid December the supplies were beginning to run low. Snow covered the mountains and the nights brought severe frosts. Although the men began to fall ill in the freezing temperatures, and his wife was still lodging at Ardea Castle, Tyrell stayed on at the camp in Glengarriff woods. Donal had sent word that King Philip was once again considering sending aid, and so there was still hope of a change of fortune.

The change turned out to be for the worse, however. The great Florence MacCarthy was arrested and taken to the Tower of London. There was no one to take his place and continue the struggle in West Cork. Lord Barry and Sir George Thornton assembled an army of over fifteen hundred, and marched from Cork to rid the south of all remaining rebels. Tyrell capitulated at last, sending his envoy Laughlin O'Dalaigh to sue for peace and agree to Carew's demand that he serve Her Majesty's forces with his men. The plea, however, was rejected. Carew was well aware that Tyrell was running out of supplies, and would soon be forced to abandon his camp. A week later Bagnall had defeated the Knight of Glen and so conquered the whole of Desmond. The struggle was at an end; Tyrell knew it now. It was time to go home.

Chapter Nine

The Final Struggle

By late December, Donal had also realised that there was very little more to be done. Confined to the Beara Peninsula his small force was in a desperate condition; sickness was rife, food was scarce and the weather was atrocious.

Lord Barry, Wilmot and Thornton had over two thousand men between them, and to stand against their three-pronged offensive there remained only a minimal, weak and hungry Irish force. Donal Cam and Burke were in Beara with five hundred men; Sir Owen MacCarthy's sons had about four hundred in West Cork, and Tyrell only three hundred and fifty, and forty horses.

When he had collected Aoife from Ardea, Tyrell entered Donal's camp on the twenty-third of December. Brushing the snow from their skin cloaks, they joined him in his tent for a bowl of hot meat stew. Donal's face was haggard and drawn, but still showed signs of some determination.

'It seems that they really mean to finish us off this time' he said, when they had eaten their meal.

'And they'll succeed, Donal. We don't stand a chance. My men are tired and sick, and I think we should give it up now; head home while we still have our lives.'

'We've come this far, Richard; surely you won't leave me now?'

'I'm sorry, my friend, but it's all over. We will be leaving in the morning.'

'Look, Richard, I need your forces. I'll give you a thousand Spanish reals, and a thousand cattle if you will fight on for another three months.'

'My mind is made up, Donal' Tyrell said quietly. 'If you offered me all the gold in Spain my answer would still be the same.'

'Then there is nothing I can say' Donal replied. He was close to tears.

Abandoning the carts, the injured and any other impediments, Tyrell and his wife and remaining men moved out with their few belongings on pack horses. They were going first to north Tipperary, where the O'Carrolls were still holding out against the English. Donal remained in his tent, and offered his friend no word of farewell.

Keeping to the high ground just below the heavy snowline, Tyrell noticed far below him a long column of soldiers with carts and gun carriages marching towards Glengarriff. He blessed himself, thanking God that they had moved out just in time.

His wife, riding beside him, said 'You always make the right decision at the right time, Richard. I hope that luck stays with us for the rest of this journey.'

'Don't worry, Aoife, I will get you home safely.' Tyrell leaned across and kissed his wife's cold cheek, and smiled.

The large, combined English force that Tyrell had seen arrived at Glengarriff and encamped not more than a mile away from Donal's base. Donal and Burke attempted an attack but were driven back by force of arms. They tried again that night, under cover of darkness, but were quickly put to flight by a barrage of gunfire and suffered heavy losses.

The wounded were being tended and the dead buried when the English, having located the enemy camp, launched their own assault. Six hundred men under Lord Barry and Captain Selby attacked at daybreak, and a vicious battle ensued. Hand-to-hand fighting broke out and lasted throughout the day, resulting in many deaths on both sides.

Pushed back by superior forces, Donal and Burke abandoned their camp and retreated further into the woods. Lord Barry ordered that all the livestock and foodstuffs be removed. With his force now heavily depleted, Donal summoned every ounce of strength left in his men and himself for a retaliation. As night was falling they drove the English back almost to their own camp, and reclaimed most of their animals in the process. Unnerved, Barry sent for two more regiments so that the camp might be secured.

Although the fighting continued until dawn, nothing more than a stalemate was achieved. With over six hundred dead on both sides and no victory now feasible, Donal's Desmond allies approached the English at noon with the intention of surrendering. Seeing them go, Burke rushed to find Donal. 'Do you know that the Desmond troops are surrendering?'

'I do. Let them go.'

'To hell I will. They are under our command and cannot surrender of their own will.'

'For God's sake William, they are only trying to save their own lives.'

'And what about our lives?' The English will overrun us within hours. No! I'll kill every one of them before I'll let them give us all up.'

Gathering his officers and remaining force of three hundred men, Burke charged into the Desmond troops, leaving over two hundred of them dead. Sickened by the carnage at last, he returned to the camp. Donal was waiting for him with a question. 'Is it all over now, William? Is that it?'

'I will never surrender, Donal. But even you must see that we have no hope as the situation stands. Either we get some assistance, or I say we pack up and try to find our way to places of safety.'

'Then we will get some assistance.'

'Where from? There will be no Spanish fleet now, you can be sure of that.'

'I know that. I'll go north, to O'Rourke and then on to O'Neill. Maybe I can convince them to fight on.'

'This is madness. How can you travel north in this weather, with many of your men wounded or sick? Connor Kerry has abandoned us now, and taken his fifty men with him.'

'I know. But we will make it. We have to.'

Burke sighed heavily. 'Very well, Donal. I won't leave you now.'

Realising that he was alone in this endeavour, apart from Burke and his two hundred or so remaining men, Donal ordered a head count. He told the men that they would be leaving as soon as darkness fell. Most believed that they would be heading west, and he didn't enlighten them at this point. There would be resistance to the plan, and he still feared the presence of spies in the camp. While he was considering the number of sick and injured men, his uncle Dermod emerged from his tent. He had himself been unwell during the past weeks, and Donal was concerned that he might not be fit for the journey. 'I am headed for O'Rourke country, Dermod. Will you join me?'

'Of course I will. I'd rather die on horseback than be cut down by an English sword. What about the rest of the family?'

'I'll leave my boy here with your wife, and my sister Síle and her husband. They can hide up in the mountains until it is safe for them to move to Muskerry or Eyeries.'

Shortly before nightfall Donal and Dermod toured the camp. They had been amazed, an hour earlier, by the return of Connor Kerry with thirty men; it was a small force, but Donal was grateful for, and moved by his offer of support. The hardest of Donal's remaining tasks was to order that the ill and injured must be left behind for the time being. Many of them pleaded and begged, insisting that they were well enough to walk, but Donal knew that they wouldn't last more than a few days in such hostile conditions. He asked them to find their way back to their homes, but was aware that many would be unable to do so. It was a sorrowful, desolate scene, and one that he never forgot.

Those left behind were told to light as many fires as possible, and any who were fit enough stood as sentries in a line between the Irish and English camps. It was Donal's intention to convince Lord Barry that his force was still in place, so that the main body of men might steal away without interception. The subterfuge was successful, and soon they were on their way.

After a week of gales and heavy rain a cold winter sun finally appeared on the thirtieth of December, and Wilmot ordered an advance on the rebel camp. As they emerged from the woods they could see nothing but a few guttering fires, and strewn around them the bodies of a few dead or dying men. Enraged, he ordered that every remaining life be ended, and when it was done he sent Lord Barry, with two regiments of light foot soldiers, to pursue Donal and his followers.

Still furious at his deception Wilmot led half of his army west through Beara, burning barns and huts, butchering animals and killing anyone that he encountered along the way. Captain Fleming was then dispatched to Dursey and Oilean Beag aboard the Merlin, with two hundred men, to root out and destroy any rebels left alive. The people of west Beara had heard of Donal's departure, and most of them had sought refuge on the islands and amongst the ruins of the castle there.

Arriving off Dursey on the eighth of January, Fleming found an old barque at anchor in a sheltered cove, along with three small sailing ships. They were immediately taken, and those aboard were killed before the task of laying waste the islands was begun.

The soldiers began to seek out every living soul. Remembering how their colleagues had been murdered by women and children as well as men in the woods of Glengarriff, they had no intention of sparing anyone. Old and young, men and women were butchered; girls were raped before being put to the sword. Some of the soldiers became so inhumanly frenzied that they were parading around with babies impaled on their spikes. Other infants were run through as they screamed in the arms of their terrified mothers. Any individuals remaining at the end of this orgy of barbarism were tied together and prodded over the edge of the cliffs at sword point, falling to their deaths on the rocks below. Satisfied that no one remained to tell the tale of this atrocity, the troops returned to their boats, and were transported on to the awaiting ships and back to Cork.

Wilmot himself had gone over the snowy mountain to attack Ardea, and after three days of cannon bombardment the castle fell. Its defenders were shot or put to the sword, and gunpowder disposed of its remains. Having been advised that the eastern route was now impassable, Wilmot decided to march back over the pass into Adrigole. It proved to be the biggest mistake of his campaign.

The troops set off towards the Claddagarriff Pass along a rough path, no more really than a donkey track. The snow began to fall more thickly, and soon they were caught in a blizzard. First they had to abandon the gun carriages, and then the carts carrying supplies. Before the head of the column had reached the pass, many of those behind had fallen down the steep mountain inclines, or collapsed by the wayside. Conditions were the worst in living memory, and more and more men fell as the day wore on. By the time a temporary camp had been established, at Inchintaglen, over three hundred men had been left for dead on the mountain.

With the weather deteriorating yet further, Wilmot gave the order to march back towards Glengarriff. It took his army two days to cover those ten miles, and another five hundred men or more were lost along the way. It was often said, in the years following these events, that God made those men pay for their unholy slaughter of the innocents.

When Wilmot finally returned to Donemark he dispatched a regiment to Carriganass Castle, which was still being held by a small group of Donal's followers. After a token resistance the defenders, about thirty in all, surrendered in the hope that their lives would be spared. Their hopes were ill founded, for they were lined up against the castle wall and shot. It was the end of the struggle for the O'Sullivans in Beara.

Chapter Ten

Abandoning Camp

Donal never looked back. He was grateful for the darkness of the night, for there were tears in his eyes. He rode at Dermod's side in silence for some time, finally uttering 'May God and the Blessed Mother protect those we have left behind. When they find us gone their vengeance will be severe.'

'There is nothing we can do now' Dermod replied. We must try and save ourselves.'

'But it was all my fault. If I had only recognised that the Spaniards wouldn't come, I could have done much more.'

'It was an impossible task, Donal. You were the victim, as soon as O'Neill and O'Donnell left us.'

'I don't know. If I had given Tyrell and Burke more support, we might have driven the English out altogether.'

'And they would have been back, with a stronger army.'

Donal nodded. 'Then maybe we should have taken that boat back to Spain.'

'No. I took a look at her, and I didn't think she was up to the journey. She won't make it across Biscay in this weather. Now we must get on; we have twenty miles to cover tonight.'

The climb out of the valley to the northeast was the first test. Most were on foot, carrying their few possessions on their backs, while the hundred or so riders took the younger children on their horses. The snow was over two feet deep in some places and capped with a crust of ice, and several people fell before they arrived at the higher ground, where the terrain was sounder. Donal moved back to the rear of the party and urged them on. Scooping an exhausted boy up onto his own horse, his heart lurched as he thought of his infant son; had his sister managed to reach the safety of a mountain cave, and would they survive in this climate anyway? If anything happened to them that, too, would be his doing.

When they reached the flat, marshy uplands of bog and grasses, Donal finally allowed himself to look back. All he could see was the glow of the fires in his own camp, and that of the English. It was hard to believe that they were so close together. Snow was encrusted on his beard, and he felt the full blast of the biting northerly wind. What horrors would the morning bring?

The long column crossed two frozen streams, having had to break the ice, and skirted Cobduff Mountain. Passing through a gorge, they entered the woods of Kealanine and then descended into the boglands. Donal was thinking that they would have been utterly lost without his two local guides, who were about to return to their homes, when a woman's screams pierced the frosty air. She had discovered that the tiny baby in her arms was lifeless, and her cries were raw and agonising. After some time, the other women managed to persuade her to part with the little body, which they wrapped up tight and laid to rest in an ancient cist grave. At least the child would not be alone, surrounded there by some of his forbearers. While the stone slabs were being replaced, Dermod offered up a few prayers. The death was to be the first of many.

By the time they had crossed the Coomhola River, the travellers were suffering the effects of the freezing cold. Only the galloglasses had single soled leather shoes, and the rest were barefoot or wearing strips of cloth on their feet. No one complained. Aware that there was still a strong English force around Carriganass, and probably guarding the pass of Ceim an Fhia, Donal had decided to follow the course of the river along its south bank into the Borlin

Valley. Then they would cross over south of the Conigar Mountain, into the north side of Gougane Barra. It was a route he had often taken in the past, when he needed to avoid detection.

Dawn arrived slowly while they were climbing the mountain in knee-deep snow. The dark clouds gathering over the hills to the west indicated that more snow would fall within a few hours, but at least it would obliterate their trail. Donal continued to exhort his followers to move faster, even though he knew that every one of them was exhausted. Dermod rode up alongside him, and they looked down through the snow-covered trees at the lake of Gougane Barra, lying placid in the morning light.

Dermod regarded the steep cliff face with anxiety. 'Which way now, Donal? If we descend here we'll surely fall to our deaths.'

'There's a long, narrow pathway running northwards, but it's only wide enough for us to go single file. And we'll have to blindfold our horses and lead them, or the drop will panic them.'

The men leading their horses went first, with those on foot following behind. They had almost reached the end of the passage when one of the horses suddenly reared up. Losing his footing he fell over the cliff face, taking the man who had been leading him with him. The sound of his screams, and the terrified neighing of the horse echoed through the valley, and many of the others were paralysed with shock for a while. Crossing themselves at last, they moved on in silence.

When they had reached the lower level, Donal called the group to a stop, to rest and eat something. He gave the order that no fires were to be lit, to avoid alerting the enemy to their presence, before setting off with a couple of men to look for their lost companion. When they located the body of the horse they removed the saddle and a bag, and looked around for a corpse. There was no body to be seen, however, and so they started to shout. 'Cormac! Cormac, are you there?'

The echoes died away, and the men shook their heads sadly, but then a muffled sound was heard. 'Cormac' they shouted again. 'Keep shouting, we'll find you!'

Scrambling up the slope towards the sound, they heard 'I'm here, stuck up here in the tree! I think my left arm and leg are broken. Christ, the pain is terrible!'

'We'll get you out, don't move!'

Half an hour later they brought Cormac down, and once on the ground he began to drift in and out of consciousness. The shinbone was sticking out of his left leg, and his arm was dangling from the elbow. Donal looked at the other men and shook his head, but they lifted him onto a hastily constructed litter and carried him back to where the rest of the group were resting. While several of them gathered around the litter, Donal spoke quietly to his uncle. 'I don't believe he's up to the journey, Dermod. All we can do is try and reset the bones, and leave him here with some food and shelter.'

One of the men overheard, and interjected 'You can't leave him here alone!'

'We have no choice' Donal replied. 'He would die before another day was out.'

The young woman whose child had died came closer. 'I will stay with him' she said. 'I have lost my husband as well as my son, and I haven't the will to go any further.'

'Very well' said Donal. 'You are a brave woman, and a kind one. We'll leave you as much food as we can, and build a shelter before we move on.'

When Cormac was told of the plan he smiled weakly. 'Ah, with this fine colleen by my side I'll be grand. Who knows what we might get up to before my time comes!'

When the travellers reached west Muskerry, where Tyrell's force had come under attack at night, the countryside was deserted. Not a living soul was in sight, not even a cow or a sheep. Only the burnt out cabins could be seen, and scorched earth showing here and there through the snow. Donal knew that sooner or later they would be seen, and urged his followers on anxiously. Dividing the horsemen, he sent some to the back in case of sudden attack, and sent out four scouts to look for any sign of danger.

By late afternoon they had arrived at the ruins of the church of Eachros, and Donal saw that they would have to make camp for the night. The people were unable to walk another mile, and many of them were too tired even to eat and slept immediately. A few small fires were lit to cook a little hot food, and as soon as the rest had eaten, and bathed their blistered feet in the stream, they too lay down. Slowly the whimpers of hungry children faded, and silence descended on the camp.

At sunrise the following day a man in a long black cloak rode into the camp on a donkey. A boy was leading the donkey, and Donal watched as the sentries let them pass. He seemed to be a priest, and indeed he introduced himself as Father Lynch. 'And this is my young helper, Padraig' he went on. 'We are on our way to Gougane Barra to say Mass, but I will stop and say a New Year's Mass for you if you wish.'

'Thank you, Father' Donal replied. 'These people would appreciate it I'm sure.'

Father Lynch conducted his service standing at the old altar stone in the ruined church, and finished with the blessing 'May God bless and protect you all throughout the long journey ahead, and deliver you from your enemies.'

Slipping a few Spanish ducats into his hand, Dermod thanked Father Lynch and asked him who lived in the cabins below in the valley.

'They are the O'Learys, relations of mine, but you will find nothing there. They have only one cow to feed eight children between them.'

'No, no, but would they help a dying man? We left him in the care of a young woman, back at Gougane Barra. He is badly injured.'

'I will find the two of them myself, and bring them back to my relations here.'

'Thank you, Father' said Dermod. 'God will reward your goodness.'

When Donal gave the signal to move out, the boy tending his

horse had taken him to graze in a piece of pasture, which was separated from the camp by a strip of bogland covered in snow. As the people began to gather up their belongings, they were startled by Donal's roar and looked up to see him charging towards the bog. Soon they realised that the boy, Jimeen, must have tried to ride the horse over the false ground into the camp. By the time they reached him he was sinking into the bog, the horse thrashing frantically beneath him with wild eyed terror. There was nothing to be done, and as horse and boy disappeared from view the women screamed and fell to their knees. Children cried out, and men blessed themselves and prayed out loud.

Before he knew what he was saying Donal shouted 'God Almighty, my fine cearc! She was the best I ever had.' Quickly, he added 'And the poor boy, Jimeen. May God bless his soul.'

Connor Kerry was beside him. 'I pointed that bog out to him only this morning, Donal. He knew he should take care there.'

Connor offered Donal the choice of his own few horses. Even though the mare he saddled now had seen better days, she was still hardy enough, and he rode around until he felt at ease on her back. Searching the landscape, he thought how different everything looked in the snow. St Gobnait's church was the nearest landmark he could remember, and he wasn't sure of the quickest route. Riding through the assembling column, he asked if there was anyone who knew the area well. Eventually a woman in her late thirties stood forward, saying 'I know the way. My mother and father made a pilgrimage to all the holy places of Ireland when I was a girl. My father made sure I remembered, God bless him, by pointing out every mountain and stream on our travels.'

Donal decided to test her knowledge. 'Where do we go from here?'

'Up along the valley, to the right through that small pass, on for a few miles and then cross over the hill and down to a small river.'

Amazed by the accuracy of her memory Donal asked 'Are you alone, woman?'

'No. I have my two sons with me here' she replied, indicating two strong boys.

'Come up ahead. I will get you a horse. I suppose you know the way to Ardpatrick?'

'I do indeed, and further to Clonmacnoise.'

The woman, whose name was Cait, pointed out every notable landmark as they rode along. It soon transpired that she was a distant relation of Donal's on his grandmother's side, one of the Clan Lawras of Adrigole.

The snow fell again as they were going through the pass of Gornabinna, but the cold wind had decreased in strength. The initial fear of being overtaken by the English force, which was doubtless following, had passed for the moment. Donal's main anxiety related to the local clans, over whose territory they were passing without permission. Most of them were subjects of Cormac MacCarthy of Muskerry, who had suffered at Tyrell and Donal's hands during the last year. Furthermore, word would now be out that Donal was carrying Spanish gold, and that there was a ransom on his head. Perhaps the bitter weather was on their side for once Donal thought, when his scouts returned without sighting any horsemen.

When they reached St Gobnait's Church, those at the front stopped and prayed for a while, to allow the stragglers to catch up up. Setting off together they headed for a nearby ford, where they would cross the River Sulane. William Burke, who was riding ahead of Donal, suddenly wheeled back to speak to him. 'There are men on horseback ahead' he said urgently.

'How many of them?'

'I saw only a dozen or so.'

'They won't trouble us if they are alone, but they may be watching us and waiting for reinforcements. We must get everyone over the river as fast as we can.'

They hadn't gone far along the bank when a shout went up from the rear. 'Horsemen and soldiers coming from the east! Two hundred or more!'

Donal swung around, feeling real fear for the first time during their journey. He didn't know how the soldiers might be armed, but they would find out soon enough.

Chapter Eleven

The First Encounter

Leaving Burke and his men to hold MacCarthy's forces for as long as he could, Donal led the rest towards the woods on the side of the hill. The first of them had reached cover when the first shots rang out behind them. The attack had begun. Burke was forced back from the open ground, and regrouped his horsemen along a line of trees. Fifty foot soldiers armed with muskets appeared, and the horses scattered into the woods as the first barrage knocked four men from their mounts and splinters flying from the trees.

A frontal attack drove Burke's men further back into the woods, but there he held his ground. Donal had brought his vanguard around, and attacked MacCarthy's soldiers on the left flank at the edge of the river. Fearing a further counter from Burke, they quickly withdrew, though not before they had rounded up some baggage animals, which had broken loose.

Donal and Burke were joined by Dermod and Connor, who asked how many they had killed.

'I counted about ten dead' Donal replied, 'And another twenty or so wounded down by the river. Did we lose any ourselves?'

'There are four men injured, two of mine and two of yours, but the women are tending to their wounds now.'

'We've seen MacCarthy's men off for a while, anyway' said Burke.

'We have, but they won't give up that easily' Donal replied.

'We must move off before they come back with reinforcements.'

'We'll head for Glendubh, along the side of Mullaghanish Mountain' Dermod interjected. 'Pursuit will be almost impossible there, and we're safe as long as we're amongst the trees here.'

Leaving Burke, Connor Kerry and their men to protect the rear, Donal and Dermod rode ahead with Cait and her sons. They led the column out of the trees and along the rough mountain path. Turning to Donal, Cait said 'Those two men of yours were O'Shea, and a MacCrehan from Dursey. One has a lead ball in his chest, the other in his stomach; they won't last long.'

'Dear God, they were good men. I'll see them when we make camp this evening. We need to make up the ground that we've lost now.'

'You know how exhausted everyone is' said Cait hesitantly. 'They're hungry too.'

'I know. I'll send a few men ahead to see if they can kill a few deer.'

'Yes, we'll need fresh meat if we're to carry on. I'm very faint myself.'

'Here' said Donal reaching back into his pack for a piece of oatmeal bread, 'Have this. It isn't much but it'll stave off the pangs until we make camp.' He watched as she divided the bread into three pieces, giving the two larger portions to her sons, and asked 'What are their names?'

'The eldest is Sean, he's fifteen, and that's Con; he's only thirteen but he's as strong as a horse.'

'They are two fine lads indeed. And what of their father?'

Cait turned on him with her eyes blazing in anger. 'You should know the answer to that question. Wasn't he the man who looked after your horse at Kinsale, shot dead during the battle!'

'Christ Almighty, you mean that you are Tadhg's widow?'

'I am indeed, and I've been tending to your uncle as well, while he was sick these past weeks. Have I not, Dermod?'

'She has, Donal, and a fine woman she is too.'

As they passed through Garranicarney they met with the full

force of a snowstorm rising from the north, and within a few minutes they were almost blinded by the blizzard. Shielding his face with his cloak, Donal peered forward but could see only a swirling mass of white and grey. He shouted to his companions to keep going, and their spirits were soon lifted when the hunters returned with four fine deer strapped to their horses. They would eat well that night at least.

Leaving the snows behind as they descended through Caumcarrig, they were now on flat land. Crossing the Finnow River, and then recrossing it further down they skirted Millstreet to the east, making camp at last in the dense woodlands of Claraghatlea North. They were only two miles from the MacCarthy castle of Drishane, so the fires they built were small. While the tents were being pitched and the deer prepared for roasting, Donal went to visit his injured men. The pallor of their skin indicated that they were on the way out, and he knelt down between them and spoke quietly. 'I am proud of you both. You have fought well, and stayed with me since Kinsale.'

'Then give us a proper burial, Donal' one of them whispered. 'Our families are already dead so there is no one else to worry about.'

Donal felt a tightness in his throat, and replied hoarsely 'Make your peace with God, my friends. He will be kind to you.' He took them both by the hand, before turning away.

A hearty, hot meal was being cooked on the fires now. Donal's two servants were suffering from frozen feet, and it was Cait and her sons that looked after the food for him and Dermod, Burke and Connor Kerry. The venison was shared equally amongst everyone there, and eaten ravenously in silence. Not a morsel was lost. The skins, however, caused problems because so many were in need of footwear. In the end the men who had killed the animals decided that they would have to draw straws, and soon a lucky few went away with their precious pieces. Cait wasn't one of them, but while her sons slept by the fire she was busy repairing their shredded footwear with thin strips of leather taken from her own shoes. She was on horseback now, and had less need of them.

There was movement in the camp well before dawn, as many were woken by the cold as soon as the fires died down. Donal was himself woken by the sound of crying and moaning not too far away. Walking around the camp, he found that three women and two men from west Beara had died in the night. Two of the women were widows of Burke's northern soldiers, and the other happened to be a friend of Cait's; somehow
they had fallen asleep without coverings, and frozen to death. They were buried amidst great sadness, and camp was broken in silence once again, but there was worse to come.

The landscape had changed, and they were in almost open country now, which brought its own problems. They could be seen from a distance, and information regarding their movements quickly relayed. Trouble could be expected at any time, and Donal posted horsemen a mile to each side and to the rear, and sent scouts out ahead. With no shelter at hand, they felt vulnerable as quarry caught in unknown territory.

The main objective for the moment was to cross An Abhainn Mór, before the MacCarthys at Drishane were alerted to their presence. Marching along the western bank of the Finnow, they reached the ford at Dromsicane, which was over fifty yards wide. A line of boulders across the river made the sand build up on the upper side, but they crossed quickly and without incident. Passing a castle seemingly unseen, they headed north to Boherbue. Apprehensive, Donal asked Cait if she was sure of the direction they were taking.

'About a mile further on you will see two large oaks, with their branches intertwined like lovers' she replied coolly.

'I'm sorry, Cait. But I am responsible for every man, woman and child here.'

'We are all responsible for each other', she said.

'Indeed' was all that Donal could say. He recognised in her the strength, but also the warmth of heart that he had loved in Ellen.

When they reached the big oaks, she cast a wry smile in his direction, and he answered it.

They decided against going into Boherbue to look for food, as the English in Limerick would probably have been told of their movements by now. Cait gave directions to Dermod, who wanted to ride ahead with twenty men, but as soon as he had departed one of Donal's scouts appeared waving his hands in the air. Alarmed, Donal yelled 'What is it?'

'Fifty, maybe a hundred horsemen riding in this direction from the north west' the scout shouted back.

'Ride back along and tell Burke and Connor, and tell the people to move closer together!' Turning to Cait, he told her to take her sons and move back into the body of the group, and then he waited.

As the horseman came over a mound and into a clearing, he could see that there were more than fifty of John Barry's men, possibly eighty of them. They too drew up, to survey the force that they had to contend with, and seemed satisfied by its apparent weakness. Sweeping in, they headed straight for the centre of the group, which was protected only by a line of pike men. When they were less than two hundred yards away, Burke and his horsemen swung around from the rear and rode in against one flank, while Donal did the same on the other side.

Barry's force tried to wheel away, but was then confronted by Dermod and his small force of twenty men. Shots were fired, and mounted hand-to-hand fighting broke out, but when Barry himself was injured he ordered a retreat. Donal gave the order to continue the march immediately. The task at hand was to cross the Allow River as quickly as possible, but Dermod reported that the ford was being held by a strong English force, and Cait knew of no other way across. There was no option but to attempt it.

Burke led the way with a hundred horsemen and about eighty men on foot, while Donal protected the rear with the remaining fifty horsemen. Over two hundred soldiers had taken up their positions on the opposite bank, and Burke could see that he wouldn't make the crossing without some losses. As a diversionary tactic he sent twenty horsemen about five hundred yards upstream to swim the river. As soon as the enemy force broke off to counteract the move, he lifted his sword and led his men roaring across the ford amid a hail of musket shot.

Assailed by what appeared to be a group of madmen, the English ranks scattered. One band of musketeers, under Captain Cuffe, tried to hold their ground but were also put to flight as soon as the foot soldiers made the crossing. Donal had gained the advantage, and the rest of his followers were hurried over the river, fifteen of them wounded, while four bodies floated away on the current. It had been a bloody crossing, but there had been no alternative.

When the injured had been seen to and a few litters made to carry them, the journey resumed once more. They were headed for the woods of Ballyhoura, where any further attacks could be more easily dealt with. Burke was particularly anxious to reach Ardpatrick, as he had stopped in that village on his march south, and knew the way north from there.

As the evening closed in Donal too was relieved that they were nearing Ardpatrick. Their many enemies now knew something of their strength, and they would not face further assault for the moment. They might though send for reinforcements; the marchers would have to keep close by the woodlands from now on. Cait said that they would soon be in Ballyhaght, an enclosed valley with dense foliage on three sides.

'Sounds ideal' Donal commented. 'We can retreat to the higher ground if attacked.'

Burke agreed. 'We cannot afford to lose any more men, Donal. That river crossing cost us, and four of the injured men have died since. Our supplies of powder and shot are low too.'

'I know, William. If the trees up ahead are suitable, we should cut some timber and make spear shafts for the women and servants; they might deter a charge at any rate.'

'We need to make camp soon' said Cait. 'Some of these people are collapsing with exhaustion and hunger.'

'I think it would be safe to send twenty men out for food now' Donal replied. 'We'll look for a suitable place to stop.'

They set up camp at the end of the small valley by the tree line. Another hard frost had already set in, and Donal ordered that fires be lit regardless of the danger. At least they would be warm, even if their stomachs were still empty. The concern now was that the men he'd sent out might have got lost in the darkness. Dermod was nowhere to be seen, and Cait told him that she'd seen Dermod riding out after the foragers.

It was well after midnight when Donal heard a short blast of a bull's horn. He knew that it was Dermod, searching for the camp. He went to his horse and grabbed his own horn from his saddlebag, gave two short blasts and heard the answering call with relief. Dermod arrived within a few minutes, dismounted and stretched his limbs. 'We were lucky', he said.

Donal looked at him questioningly. 'How lucky?'

'We all came back alive, didn't we?'

'Stop your rameshing, Dermod. What did you find?'

There was a pause, and then he replied 'I'm sorry, but I had to use some of your Spanish gold.'

'I don't care about that. Tell me what you got!'

'I got enough to feed everyone here. Three cows, eight pigs, a few banabheens, some barley and ten bags of oats.'

'God Almighty, you did well!'

'And not a word of thanks' Dermod smiled.

As late as it was, the fires were rekindled and the food cooked and portioned out. With their hunger satisfied at last, men, women and children lay down by the blazing fires to sleep for a while. It was a rare night of content in the midst of that long, cold winter.

Chapter Twelve

Running Battle

With over twenty miles of open countryside to cover before they could reach the woods of Slieve Felim Mountain, they were on their way well before dawn broke. As far as Burke was concerned this was potentially the most dangerous part of the journey, as they would be passing within eight miles of Limerick. They marched in a state of readiness for attack, using the same formation as before; Donal and Connor took the rear with forty of their best men, while William and Dermod led the way and outriders flanked the column a mile or so out.

Passing to the west of Ardpatrick in the cold, bright morning light, William Burke spotted two riders about a mile and a half ahead. A message was sent back to Donal, and the pace hastened. The ground was still crusted in frost and ice, and Cait was concerned that some of the people were too weak to walk any faster.

'We have no choice' Donal shrugged. 'We are in open country here and need to move on quickly.'

'Do you think we'll be attacked again today?'

'It's very likely. Lord Barry, the White Knight, will not let us escape so easily. He's probably been gathering a force since yesterday.'

'I've nothing to defend myself with.'

'Your sons have timber spikes. Here, have this' he said, reaching back into his bag for a long knife.

'Thank you, Donal.'

'If we are attacked move in amongst the baggage horses, and take Con and Sean with you.'

The fast pace was taking its toll; by the time they reached the village of Hospital five women and some children had fallen by the wayside, unable to carry on. Donal could do nothing but bless them as he passed. Out in front, Burke and Dermod received the message that a large force was coming in from the west and would intercept them near a hill about two miles ahead. The force, said the rider, was over three hundred strong including mercenaries. It could be a disastrous battle, but there was no way out; they must walk into it.

Not knowing whether the force would make a frontal attack or wait to locate the weakest section of the group, Burke took a gamble. He sent word back that the foot soldiers should march in single file at both sides of the column, and everyone armed with a timber spear position themselves between the soldiers and the main group, women and youths included. This would give the impression that their own force was at least twice as strong as it was, and might make the enemy hesitate.

The White Knight's army marched in until they were almost parallel, about half a mile to the west. After their previous encounter they were no doubt in a state of some apprehension regarding the strength of Donal's force, and trying now to assess it. A kind of stalemate ensued, and might have continued were it not for the collapse of two of the marchers. When cornered and interrogated by Lord Barry's men, they admitted that a large part of the weaponry consisted of timber spikes. A short time later the onslaught began, with Barry's force breaking into two sections and mounting forays on both sides, knowing that the marchers and baggage would have to be protected at all costs. Leaving twelve men at the rear Donal moved up with the rest while Burke came down, leaving some of his horsemen to forge the way ahead with Dermod.

The horsemen, who had been ordered to fire their muskets

only when a shot would guarantee serious injury, countered sporadic attacks by their opposite numbers well enough. It was a different story, though, when spears came hailing down on the mass of marchers; with little or no protection many of them fell to the ground. Donal was aware that the White Knight could have reinforcements coming in, and gave the order to increase the pace once again so that they might cross the small river ahead without being cornered. Observing the manoeuvre Barry's horsemen rode ahead, leaving their mercenaries and foot soldiers unprotected. Donal and Burke seized the opportunity to launch an attack, and although it was short lived they inflicted heavy losses, and lost only two of their own men. Their action also had the effect of bringing the enemy horseman back, which gave the marchers the time they needed to cross the river with all of the baggage, and the wounded on litters. Donal doubled his force at the rear, and managed to shrug off any who came in pursuit.

The skirmishing continued throughout that wintry day, until it became a kind of running battle with many falling on both sides. Soon, Donal was forced to exhort those carrying the wounded or exhausted to abandon them and keep running. Looking behind at his followers being butchered where they fell his blood burned with impotent fury, but there was nothing to be done.

As they approached the Slieve Felim woods darkness fell suddenly, as the skies clouded heavily under their burden of snow and sleet. They were relieved to see the White Knight's forces drawing off; it had cost them dearly, but they were safe for now. Dermod found a secure location for their camp that night at an ancient stone fort, Soloheadbeg or Rath Ui Bheara, and guided the marchers into its confines. Branches and brushwood were cut, with which to fortify the crumbling perimeter walls and build a few fires. Everyone was crowded in together with the animals, and for once the cold would not trouble them too much, but their hunger would. The last of the oats had gone to the horses, there was nothing left, and the day had been a hard one.

Donal could not refuse the request of Cait and some of the other women to go in search of berries and roots. His own stomach ached with emptiness and he felt faint and light headed. All around him children were crying for food, and injured men moaned. Burke told him that over twenty soldiers and fifty marchers had been lost on that one, terrible day.

'We'll none of us reach Leitrim, William, if it goes on like this' Donal replied.

'We might if we could eat' Burke muttered grimly.

'At first light tomorrow we'll go out foraging. Is there a village nearby?'

'Donohill fort is a few miles away, I think, but it won't be easy to get anything there. From what I remember the place is well defended.'

'But we have to try, William.'

'Right. We must take the best men we have, Donal. I'll see you in the morning.'

Unable to sleep with the hunger gnawing at his stomach, Donal wrapped himself up tightly and went out to sit by the fire. The women were returning in the darkness, and as they came closer he saw Cait coming towards him with a bundle of roots in her arms.

'Look' she said, 'I'll try and make some soup with these.'

'Feed yourself and your boys' Donal replied. 'Don't worry about me.'

'And who will lead us if you fall ill?'

'Alright, Cait, thank you.'

The four of them ate the meagre meal, which contained little nourishment but was warm and very welcome. They lay down to sleep for a few hours then. The boys seemed to be reliving the terrors of the day in their dreams, for they cried out and flinched again and again.

The sky was still black when Dermod roused his nephew. 'Come on, Donal. I think we must raid that fort at Donohill before sunrise if we are to succeed. If we don't find some food the march is over.'

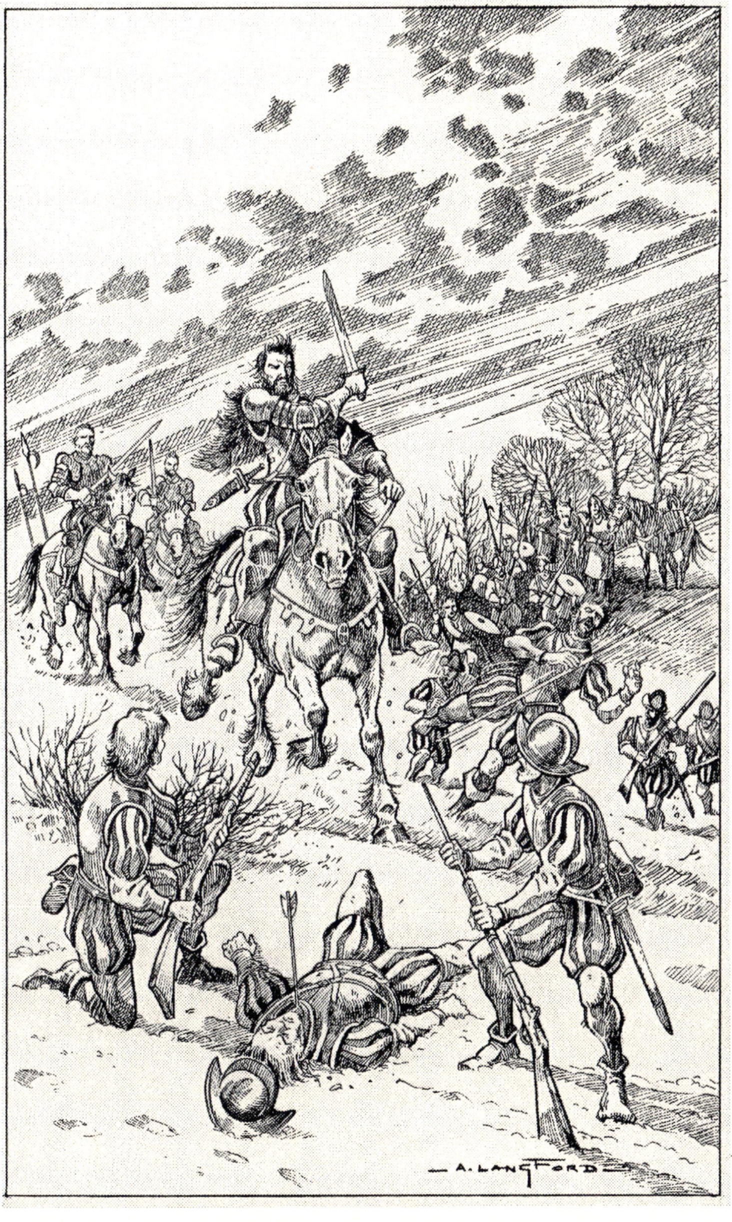
A. LANGFORD

Donal sat up shakily. 'Is Burke ready to go?'

'I think so. I saw him saddling his horse a short while ago.'

'Right, I'll join him now. You and Connor can gather the people and lead them out.'

'Would you not prefer me to come with you?'

'No, Dermod, the people need you with them. And there'll be plenty more excitement for you before this trip is out.'

Word had reached the fort at Donohill that Donal was in the area, and during the night its inhabitants had been busy concealing themselves and their food supplies. Reinforcements had been sent for, extra defensive precautions taken and the livestock driven into the woods under guard. When two scouts returned to Donal with this information his heart fell, and he had to consider calling off the raid.

'We can't do that, Donal' said Burke. 'These people must eat, today.'

He thought for a moment. 'Then we'll split our force and attack from opposite sides. I'll come in first, from the west, and as soon as they engage you can move in from the east, with the advantage of the falling ground.'

With the men driven on by the power of their hunger, the attack was launched. Burke's men were driven back at first, but Donal pushed in regardless and gained entry from the east. Burke came in after him, and the battle descended into carnage as the occupants of the fort risked their lives to defend their supplies. An ordinary foraging raid had become a bloodbath, and Donal could hardly believe the scene before him as he sat back on his horse at last. They had overcome the defensive force, and would eat that day, but at what cost? All around him lay the bodies of men, women and even children, Irish people like himself, who had wanted only to guard against their own starvation. Some of his men lay dying too, comforted by their companions who seemed to be in a stunned daze. Suddenly and violently sickened, he wheeled his horse around and rode away from the sight of it. There had, he thought bitterly, been no victory here.

The search for food commenced, but very little could be found. It had been hidden too well, and only a few bags of oats and a small quantity of barley were located. Two men who uncovered some oaten bread were so hungry that they ate it immediately, without thought for anyone else. While the wounded were being collected, some of the surviving inhabitants were questioned about the location of the hidden supplies. But despite being threatened with death none would reveal it. Burke came in search of Donal, who sitting on his horse looking out into the distance. 'They were a costly few bags of food, my friend.'

Donal looked up. 'How many have we lost?'

'Twelve dead and some twenty injured, eight of them seriously. Six horses are down, too.'

'And the food we have will feed only thirty or forty, with still so far to go.'

'We'll have to find more, somehow. The men are ready to move out now.'

'Right, William. See that the dead are promised a Christian burial.'

Donal rejoined his uncle at the head of the column, and they marched on. Glancing around, he asked 'Where are Padraig and his brother?'

'Padraig is dead, Donal. He got the full blast of a musket shot in the chest, God rest his soul. Jeremiah was spiked in the leg; he should be able to ride again within a day or two. '

'What a waste, Dermod, all for nothing.'

'We weren't to know. We'll find something else, God willing.'

By midday there was still no sign of any enemy movement, and Donal allowed the pace to slacken while two groups of four riders went out in search of provisions. They soon returned, however, saying that they had seen two forces of over fifty men coming towards then from the north. One of the riders thought that he recognised them as the O'Dwyers and O'Ryans, who had plundered O'Neill's forces as they retreated northwards. Dermod looked at Donal. 'What now?'

'If we can break them up, before they get any closer, we might stand a chance' Donal replied. 'Fetch Burke and his men to me here.'

'Why can I not go with you?'

'Oh Dermod, one of us has to stay alive.'

The enemy force, which was made up mostly of foot soldiers with pikes, had drawn up in two lines expecting to be attacked from the front. Donal and Burke took their men around to the rear of them and came in from both sides. Surprised, the soldiers scattered into the nearby woods, seeking shelter from the horsemen. A few were cut down as they ran but then Donal, who had seen enough bloodshed of late, called off his men.

Pushing on northwards they were crossing rough and wooded terrain now, and soon had to force their way through undergrowth in search of the path. As they struggled along they came suddenly face to face with the O'Dwyer and O'Ryan forces once more. The foliage was too thick to allow for horsemen, and Donal had to employ his foot soldiers, whose numbers had dwindled, to stave off the random attacks. Not until they emerged on open ground were the enemy driven away at last.

They made camp at Hollyford before the darkness came down that night. Weak and dispirited, the marchers would go no further. Dermod almost fell from his horse, and as he watched the meagre rations being spooned out his temper flared. 'We must do something Donal' he growled. 'No one will have the strength to move out in the morning.'

'You don't have to tell me that, but we must wait until tomorrow. It's just too dangerous to send men out now. There is a stream here at least; we'll have to fill our bellies with water for now.'

Too hungry to sleep, the people searched in the gloom for anything they could eat, some even resorting to the bark of the trees or slugs buried deep in the cold earth. It seemed though that some were being troubled by a hunger of a different kind. Donal was horrified, when he passed his uncle's tent, to hear the muffled sounds of a woman's cries. Pulling back the skins he saw Dermod trying to pin Cait down with one hand, his other hand over her mouth. Roaring furiously, Donal grabbed his uncle's tunic and wrenched him away from the terrified woman, letting her run away under the cover of the darkness. 'Hell, man' he shouted, 'Will you never give up those ways?'

'I thought she was willing earlier on' muttered Dermod, his eyes lowered.

'Ah get to your bed, old man' was all Donal said to him.

Donal paced the camp all that night, rousing the collapsing sentries with promises of food. They could rest as much as they wanted, he told them, when they reached O'Rourke's country. He understood it was only about forty miles away, he said, but he was thinking that at that moment it seemed to him further away than the stars in the black night sky.

Chapter Thirteen

Desperation

Cait woke Donal with a handful of grass and nettles. 'This is all we could find' she said. 'Some more children died in the night. The situation is desperate.'

'Burke and his man O'Malley are going out at daybreak with their fittest remaining men' he replied. 'We won't move until they return with some food.'

Donal felt too weak to move, and could only wish Burke and his men luck in their expedition. 'Don't take any chances' he warned them. 'O'Dwyer and O'Ryan will probably still be watching us. But for God's sake don't come back with nothing. We can go no further without nourishment.'

'I know, Donal. We'll do our best.'

There was nothing to do but wait. The small fires were kept alight so that at least the weak and starving wouldn't freeze, and sentries remained on the perimeters of the camp. Some were posted a mile or so outside, so that those who wished to search for roots or grubs could do so without immediate fear of attack.

The day passed agonisingly slowly, but still there was no sign of Burke's party. Donal and Dermod began to feel apprehensive, and the wives who had been left at the camp were fearful for their husbands' lives. Dermod felt that they must take action. 'Something has gone wrong' he said.

'I'll take a few men out' Donal replied as he mounted his horse, 'But I can't leave the camp unprotected.'

'Then go now. There isn't much light remaining.'
'Which direction did they take, Uncle?'
'West, I think.'
'To the west' Donal shouted to his small group of men, and then spurred on his mount.

They searched the countryside, but there was no sign of Burke and O'Malley anywhere. As the darkness fell they reined up on a small hill, and Donal scanned the surrounding terrain. 'God damn it! Where are they?'

One of his companions, who had a slightly better view, turned suddenly towards him. 'What's that?'

'What?'

'Look there, it's a man running this way from the north.'

Swivelling around, Donal exclaimed 'Almighty God, it looks like Burke! What in the hell is going on?'

When he saw Donal's party riding towards him, Burke stopped and waved his arms before sinking breathless to the ground. Dismounting at his side Donal demanded 'What has happened? Where are the others?'

Burke lifted his head and shook it. 'All dead, as far as I know.'

Donal was astounded. 'What? How?'

Still fighting for breath Burke went on 'We divided our men when we were about two miles outside of the camp. I went northwards, while O'Malley headed towards the Shannon. I think it was the O'Dwyers that attacked us; they must have been reinforced, and they quickly cut us down. I was taken prisoner and tied to my horse, but I managed to escape when they left to join the O'Ryans, who were tracking O'Malley and his men. They must have been ambushed, for I found their bodies on my way here.'

Speechless for a moment, Donal sat down. 'All of them, dead?'

'Every one.'

'Some of them had wives and children back at the camp.'

'They did, Donal. Seven of my men, and I think three of yours.'

'How are we going to explain their deaths? And how can we go on with so many lost, and still nothing to eat? We'll never reach O'Rourke's castle. We are finished, William, finished.'

The two men looked at one another, and said nothing more.

Donal pulled Burke up on to his own horse, and they rode back to the camp through the darkness. The people gathered round, hoping for food at first but soon realising that something was desperately wrong. One woman rushed forward shrieking 'Where is my husband?'

'Hush, woman' said Donal. 'There was nothing we could do. The riders were ambushed and vastly outnumbered, and though they fought bravely all of them were killed except Captain Burke here, who was taken prisoner.'

The woman dropped to her knees and began tearing at her hair and wailing, and all of the other bereaved women and children soon joined in. Grief overcame the camp, and all thoughts of hunger were temporarily forgotten.

Donal sat down near a fire next to Dermod, who asked him what he planned to do now.

'I don't know, Uncle. We have less than three hundred fighting men left between all of us, and we are only half way to Leitrim. There is nothing to eat and the people are starving to death. What can we do?'

'Surely we have to keep going? If we stay here we will all be killed anyway. I have no intention of letting my bones rot in this God-forsaken part of the country.'

'I don't know how we can carry on . . .' Donal began but was interrupted by the rising voices of two women nearby, one of whom was accusing the other of stealing some of her roots while she was tending the fire.

'I didn't go near your damned food' she spat back.

'You must think I'm blind! Didn't I see you with my own two eyes?'

'Go to hell!'

'I have a child to feed, you thief! Give those roots back to me!'

'I will not' said the woman, and her accuser fell on her screaming and tearing at her face and clothes. Donal stood up, appalled at the depths to which these people had sunk in the course of his work. Pulling them apart he shouted 'Stop it now! Stop!'

Struggling, the first woman said 'But she has my roots!'

'Right, then she'll give them back to you.' He let go of the woman who had stolen the tiny tubers, and watched as she flung them on the ground. The other knelt down in the darkness and searched the earth for them, and Donal felt that this must be the lowest point of his life.

Fearing another attack when daylight came, Donal gave the order to march out. Burke and O'Connor agreed that the camp was not suitable for defensive purposes, and that they should at least move on. The people walked slowly, reluctantly. One widow, whose three children had been buried at the camp, refused to leave their graveside.

Despite Donal's urging the pace was extremely slow. Every step was an effort, and the thaw that had set in recently added to their difficulties as the frozen snow gradually turned to slush. Those at the end of the column were wading through a cold and dirty quagmire. Soon after they set off the starving marchers began to drop away; mostly women and children, and then some soldiers too. Donal knew that his band of followers was dwindling by the hour, but there was nothing he could do.

By the time they made camp that evening, near the church of St Odhran's, over fifty had fallen by the wayside. The garrisoned castle of the de Mariscos was within their sights, but most were unable to walk another step. O'Connor and Donal set off with ten horsemen, and were blessed by an encounter with a goods cart on its way to the castle. The cart had no armed escort, and the driver and his boy were easily overcome and sent running through the woods. They headed back to the camp with several bags of oats and barley.

Their arrival sent the camp into uproar, as the supplies were hastily portioned out and set to cook on the fires. Donal sent warning around that they should eat slowly, but hunger drove many to cram the hot porridge into their mouths and shrunken stomachs. They burnt their tongues and coughed or retched, and the sight of mothers trying to feed their emaciated children was heart rending when the infants were simply unable to consume the food, but most managed to take some nourishment. There would be enough for the following day, too, and after a few hours' rest they were able to rise up and set off once more.

Not far into their journey they saw a strong group of riders, whom Donal understood to be from the de Marisco castle, closing in on them from the rear. He regrouped his horsemen at the back of the column and waited for an assault, but none came. The riders maintained their distance, and Burke rode back to consult Donal. 'What do you think?'

'I don't know. They're strong enough to attack us, certainly.'

'Maybe they are just seeing us off, or maybe they are waiting for the right place, or there might even be reinforcements coming in front of us.'

'Yes; we'd better take precautions. You take some men and go ahead, and for God's sake stay alert.'

Burke had no sooner disappeared from sight than the de Marisco force launched their assault from the rear. Donal brought back his pike men and lined them up across the flat ground while he divided his few horsemen and placed them at both ends, with a reserve of eight in the centre.

As soon as the enemy horsemen came within about sixty yards they drew up, as if hesitating. They were clearly unaccustomed to seeing an Irish force arranged in this manner, and recognised the danger that they were in. After feigning a few attacks and discharging a few musket shots they withdrew.

The de Marisco force returned to their earlier position behind Donal, making halfhearted attempts at assault at random intervals. Dermod rode beside his nephew, asking 'What are they doing, trying to slow us down?'

'They are, I think' Donal replied, 'But they are also hoping to pick off our men one by one. Two men are dead and three injured already.'

Dermod pointed at the wood ahead of them. 'Why not give them a surprise when we get in there? It might drive them off.'

'Well it's worth a try', Donal replied as Burke returned to his side.

As soon as they entered the forest, Donal's foot soldiers concealed themselves in the foliage on both sides of the path with pikes and swords. Donal and Burke massed their riders further in, and then they waited. De Marisco's men rode right into the ambush, and were forced to retreat in disarray. They left ten men dead behind them, and would give the marchers no further trouble then or on any other day.

Having avoided the O'Kennedy castle at Lackeen, the marchers came to a stop late that afternoon and set up camp at the old Lorrha monastery. Intent on crossing the Shannon as soon as possible Donal sent four men of Burke's men, who knew the location of the boats, to see if it was safe to approach.

When the scouts returned with the news that there were no boats within three miles of the river, Donal guessed that the High Sheriff, Donnchadh MacEgan of Redwood Castle, had been alerted to his presence and sent all the vessels downstream. The MacEgans were only four miles to the north, doubtless with a sizeable force, and with the O'Kennedys a few miles to the east he felt trapped. Burke, too, said that it was only a matter of time before they were attacked.

Donal replied 'But what can we do? What about going up this side of the river?'

'No, Donal. Athlone is only thirty miles away, and there'll be a garrison there of over five hundred soldiers. With our present force we wouldn't last an hour.'

'Do you have any plan, then?'

William looked at Donal, and a silence ensued.

It was broken by Dermod, who said 'We will build some boats to take us over the river.'

Donal looked doubtful. 'How do we do that?'

'Leave it to me' said Dermod, turning and walking quickly away.

Chapter Fourteen

The Crossing

As dawn broke, about forty men and twenty women were tramping into the wood closest to the river. Dermod told the men to cut down all the saplings, and the women to gather the reeds on the bank, and took four men away with him to one side of the wood. There they cleared a patch of ground, where he measured out a distance with his feet and marked it with straw rope strung between two poles. As he drew the outline of a boat in the earth, it was obvious that he had planned his enterprise well.

The workers used their swords and their knives to fashion a long piece of wood into a keel, which was suspended between the two markers. Half gunnels were formed, and joined with timber plugs, and the vessel began to take shape. Dermod himself was working on the oars, so that he could move around and show the others what to do. Burke and his men, meanwhile, had begun work on a smaller boat further along the riverbank.

When Donal, Burke and Connor Kerry arrived later that day they were astounded by the progress that had been made, but also enraged by the scene laid out before their eyes. Dermod and his workers were sitting around a roaring fire, feasting on the remains of two young does that they had found drinking at the riverside. Incredulous, Donal demanded 'Why did you not bring this fresh meat back to the camp?'

Dermod finished the piece he was chewing on and then

replied 'We have boats to build here. It is hard work and unless we have food to sustain us the project is doomed.'

Donal could not at first respond; he knew that his uncle was right. 'All right' he said at last, 'But if you find more you'll have to share it out among the rest of us.'

'We will, Donal, we will. Now we must get back to our work, the light is fading fast.'

Back at the camp, Donal went round to strengthen the sentries. There was very little that he could do, and he knew that he was dependent upon his uncle to get them out of this desperate situation before they were all killed, or died of starvation.

When he got back to his little hide tent, his two servants were nowhere to be seen. Assuming that they had deserted he was trudging across the camp, swearing to himself, when he saw Cait and her sons by the fire. She was cooking some bit of food, while they were sharpening some timber spikes. 'Here' said Cait without lifting her head, 'There's a small bite of food for you.'

'Thank you, Cait. Do you know where my two men are?'

'Someone said that they'd gone down to the river to help your uncle. Did you not see them there?'

'I did not, but it was getting dark.'

'Forget them now, sit down and eat.'

Donal drank down the bowl of gruel, and wiped it out meticulously with his finger. 'My God, I was so hungry; you are a good woman. Did you have something yourselves?'

'We had a little, yes. Donal . . .' Cait hesitated, 'I want to thank you for what you did for me the other night.'

'Ah no, it isn't worth mentioning' Donal replied, aware of her uneasiness.

'But it is. That uncle of your has a fierce lust on him sometimes, and I was too weak to fight back.'

'You would think he's had enough at his age wouldn't you' Donal smiled, 'After siring seventeen children or more. He's worse than an old ram.'

Cait's boys had wrapped themselves in their skins and fallen asleep, but she and Donal talked on into the night. Placing some sticks on the fire, she said to him 'You must miss Ellen very much.'

Donal thought for a moment. 'I do of course, but there's little room for memories on a battlefield.'

'I hear that she was a fine woman. It was a terrible shame for her to die that way.'

'She must have gone mad when she realised she would never see our son again' Donal replied musingly.

'Is your boy safe now?'

'I can only hope and pray that he is safe with my sister and her husband. I'll hear nothing for a while yet.'

'God willing, he is' said Cait as she got to her feet. 'I must go and lay my head down now.'

'Good night to you, woman.'

As she was leaving, Cait turned back. 'If you ever needed some company, Donal . . . I wouldn't give you the same reception that I gave your uncle.'

Thoughts of Ellen were crowding Donal's mind, and he said nothing but looked into Cait's strong blue eyes, and then she was gone.

Down by the river the following day, Dermod had almost finished the frame of his boat, and decided to go and take a look at how Burke's work was progressing. He was surprised to see that instead of resembling a curragh, it was almost circular in shape. Looking enquiringly at William he said 'Why did you not copy the design of mine?'

'This is the only kind I know how to build' Burke replied. 'It's the type we use up north on the lakes.'

Dermod shook his head. 'Well you won't be dealing with a lake down there; it's a fast flowing river. You'll never be able to control her.'

'We'll see' said Burke.

'We will. Now, I need some horses killed.'

'You need what?'

'We need skins, man, to sheet the boats. And if we don't get across the river we'll all die here, won't we? Men and horses alike!'

Despite their owners' objections, seven horses were slaughtered, and the work of skinning them begun before they were cold. The scouts had reported that a sizeable force was moving down slowly from MacEgan's castle, and time was now the enemy.

The cleaned skins were measured out into suitable lengths, with any discarded pieces being cut into strips with which to secure the frame. Sap was collected from the trees, so that it could be mixed with mud to seal the joining and stitching. They worked at a feverish pace until both boats were finished. Some men stopped to eat a piece of the cooked horseflesh, but nobody from Beara would touch it despite their hunger; there was an old saying in the region that anyone who did would die roaring.

By late evening the camp was almost surrounded, and time had run out. A few servants and the remaining women stayed to keep the fires burning, which would fool MacEgan for a while, and the rest prepared to move out. Under cover of darkness Donal and Dermod led the way down to the river where the boats were waiting, well hidden amongst the rushes. The larger one departed first, carrying the fittest remaining soldiers, and then Burke's vessel was launched. Those on the bank could only watch in dismay as a few minutes later it capsized, throwing its eight occupants into the water. They cried out for help, but were quickly taken under by the rapid current, and disappeared. The horses they had been towing swam away, taking whatever baggage they had on their backs with them. Soon all that could be seen in the half-light was the outline of the upturned coracle, bobbing downstream.

'Hell' Dermod exclaimed, 'I told that idiot that the boat wasn't up to these waters.'

'Well there's nothing we can do about it now' Donal replied. 'We must concentrate on getting the others across before MacEgan realises what we're doing.'

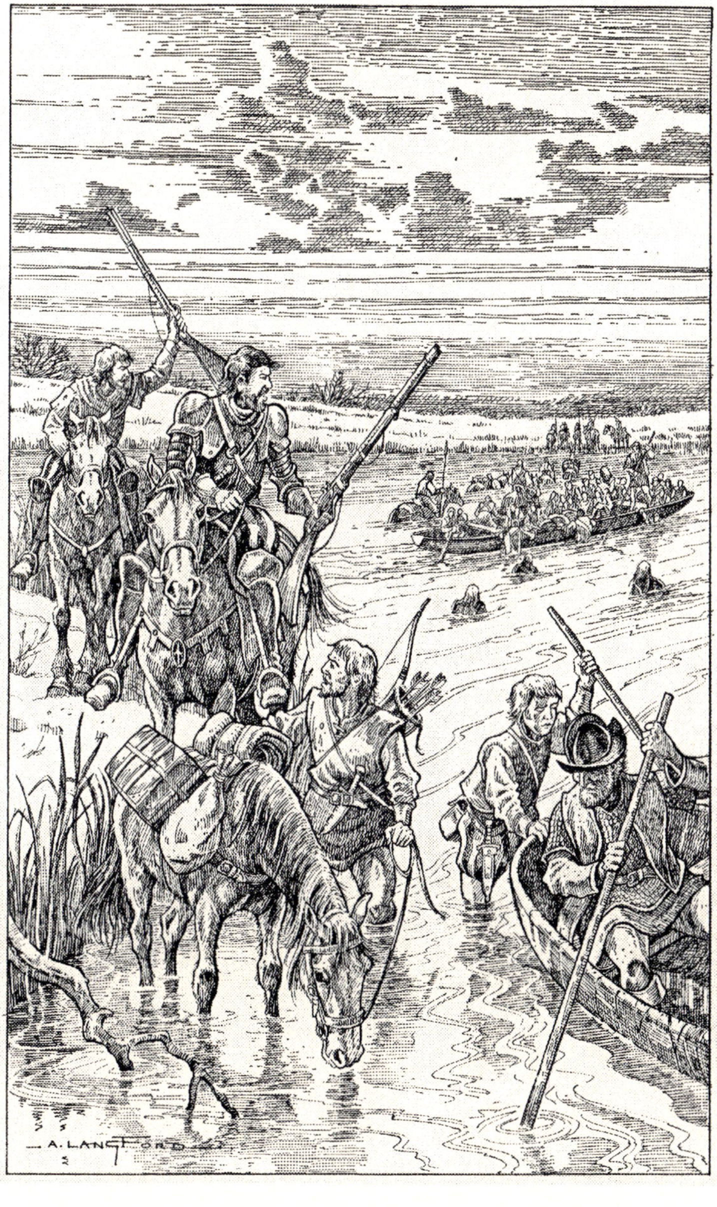
A. LANGFORD

Screaming and shouting from behind told them that the camp had been attacked. 'We have to get everyone across, now! Take charge of the boat yourself, will you Dermod?'

'Alright, but you'll have to try and hold MacEgan's men back somehow.'

'I'll send Burke back to defend our rear, but we can't afford to engage with them now.'

Burke rode out with his men to protect some of the women, who had abandoned the camp at last and were being pursued by some foot soldiers. When they arrived at the riverbank they reported that MacEgan's men had killed some of the other women and most of the baggage horses.

'We'll have to start swimming the rest of the horses across with the next boat load' Donal said. 'We won't manage on the other side without mounts. Has anyone here seen Cait?'

There was no reply, and Donal set off to find her so that he could see her safely across. While he was searching in the darkness he heard Burke a couple of hundred yards away, shouting an order to attack. At first he cursed such impulsiveness, but so strong was the desire to get everyone across the river that William's men launched themselves at MacEgan's far superior force with fresh ferocity. Over twenty were killed on the first charge, including MacEgan himself.

The enemy was not to be deterred, however, and under MacEgan's second-in-command they rallied with their own assault, eventually driving Burke and his men back towards the river. Panic broke out on the bank, and people fought to board the incoming boat. Hopelessly overloaded it struggled away from the riverside, with men and women still trying to jump on board and pulling at its sides, until it too capsized throwing every passenger into the icy water.

The scene in the river was one of mayhem, as people grasped at each other or anything moving in an effort to stay afloat. Somehow the boat was returned to the bank a few hundred yards further downriver, righted, and filled this time in an orderly manner. Most of the passengers reached the other bank, though some were swept away.

Upriver, MacEgan's men were cutting down those left behind as they ran or tried to swim for safety. Burke's force was now joined by Donal, who had been unable to find Cait, but they were losing ground fast. When the empty boat came back they ordered everyone left into it, and any who couldn't fit in to hold on to the pieces of sugán rope hanging over the sides. Donal and Burke and their horsemen urged their horses into the water, and crossed the river themselves.

When he reached the other side, Donal enquired after Cait once again. No one had seen her since she had climbed into the boat, telling her two boys to hold on to the ropes and swim across. People were already sinking in the mud on the riverbanks as they tried to haul others in from the water, and Donal decided to get back into the curragh and look for her in the river itself. When he found her she was flailing around and screaming out the names of her sons.

'Take my hand' said Donal as they came alongside, and he hauled her up beside him.

'My boys, Donal! Where are they?'

'Where did you last see them?'

'They were hanging on to the boat, and I turned away for a minute and when I looked back they were gone.'

'Calm yourself, Cait, and tell me can they swim?'

'The eldest only. Oh God, no, oh Donal don't say they've drowned.'

'We'll go down stream and look for them.'

They searched the freezing water for over half an hour, and although they managed to pull five half-drowned men out there was no sign of Sean or Con. Donal knew, at any rate, that no one would survive those temperatures for long. Cait was inconsolable, sitting on the floor of the boat crying uncontrollably. Donal tried to comfort her, but there was very little he could say to give her any hope.

When they finally regrouped on the western bank the sun was rising, and the true extent of the losses became clear. Of the five hundred who had made camp three nights previously, only three hundred or so survived. The dead were mostly women, children and servants, though dozens of fighting men were lost too in the MacEgan attack. Sean and Con, it seemed, must be counted among them.

When the curragh had been torched, to prevent it being used by the enemy, the remaining marchers were placed in some kind of order and moved off once more. Barely half an hour into their journey, however, they were set upon by the O'Maddens. It was a small force, interested mostly in booty, and after a few skirmishes they were driven off. The exhausted marchers had been forced to run for open ground to lose them though, and it was not a good beginning.

Donal thought that maybe their luck had changed at last, when they came across a village that had been recently deserted. Fires were still burning and there was enough food there to feed them all, come nightfall. For now they would have to keep moving; all of the countryside would know of their presence now, and of the direction in which they were heading.

Even though they had only twenty horses now, including five packhorses, they made good time that morning, still fearful of looting attacks. Donal's Spanish gold was safe, divided between two of the baggage horses, which were guarded by ten galloglasses.

Falling back to where Cait was walking as if in a daze, Donal reached out his hand. 'Come and ride with me.'

Looking up at him with swollen, red eyes she muttered 'Thank you', and let him swing her up behind him. She clung on to his waist fiercely, and he could feel the desperation in it, but said nothing for the moment.

They had covered about four miles in silence, when Cait spoke at last. 'I was about to give in, Donal, when you came back for me. I didn't want to keep going any more.'

'There's still hope, Cait. The boys might have made it to the bank further upstream, and if they did they're well able to look after themselves.'

Cait didn't answer him. After a while she began to cry again, and she didn't stop. They rode on together, into the day.

Chapter Fifteen

Further Danger

Everyone ate well that night. The smelly and blood splattered clothes were washed, and dried by the fires, supplies were checked and shot and muskets counted and cleaned. The people worked in silence though, taking stock also of how many had been lost. A pall of grief hung heavily in the air.

His servants having disappeared or been killed, Donal had nobody to serve him. Cait still walked around as if oblivious to her surroundings, but she managed to look after a few of the remaining horses and the food for Donal, Dermod, Burke and Connor Kerry. As the men sat around a fire after their meal that night, Donal asked William 'How many fighting men have we left?'

'Two hundred and thirty; about two hundred galloglasses and kerns, and thirty horsemen including ourselves. But as you know, we haven't enough horses. Some of those we have are too sick or lame to be ridden.'

'It's bad, but we have to keep going. Our enemies are doubtless gathering their troops, preparing to intercept us tomorrow.'

'It's open country we're heading into, Donal; escape will be difficult.'

'And we don't have enough arms for everyone. We'll have to make more timber staves and clubs, so at least the people can try and defend themselves.'

A bitterly cold northerly wind greeted them the following

morning. Seeing the dark clouds massing to the north Dermod commented 'More snow on the way.'

Donal looked up. 'When?'

'Tomorrow at the latest.'

'Then we must be on our way. I'll give the signal now.'

Apprehensive of attack at any moment, Donal posted William and Connor with one hundred galloglasses as a vanguard. They were followed by the scattering of servants, three remaining women and five baggage horses. Donal brought up the rear with Dermod beside him, and the rest of the galloglasses and kerns. Five men with minor injuries were carried on litters, but those more seriously ill or wounded were left behind.

Although scouts had been dispatched, they were surprised about four hours into their journey when soldiers emerged from the trees on both sides of their path, and drew up in battle formation.

'God Almighty' Burke exclaimed, 'They're English! Where did the bastards come from?'

Connor looked anxiously at the troops, which now stretched out over six hundred yards. 'What are we going to do?'

'Well we can't run. Pass the word back to Donal, and ready yourself.'

'How many do you think there are?'

'There are five or six companies of foot soldiers there, and two troops of horsemen. That's well over a thousand men I'd say, more . . . Christ, they're advancing. Give the word!'

Behind them, the servants and women had drawn themselves into a small circle, armed with spikes and with the packhorses shielding them. Some of the men at the front panicked when they saw the huge force bearing down, and ran for the rear where Donal was positioned on the higher ground. 'Fall in' he roared. 'We must hold our line! If they think we are afraid we'll all die here!'

As the troops advanced slowly, Donal placed two rows of kerns at the front, armed with darts and spears. As soon as the enemy was within striking distance they fired every missile simultaneously, and many of their targets fell dead or wounded. Still they came forward though, moving almost mechanically and five or six lines deep.

Ordering the kerns to fall back, Donal brought the galloglasses forward in their chain mail, armed with swords and axes and backed up by the kerns, carrying swords now and even a few shields. 'For Ireland', he shouted to embolden the men he knew to be capable of great bravery, despite their weaker state 'Avenge Kinsale!'

They fought like men possessed but were forced back by the pressure of numbers, and after the first onslaught had to fall back and regroup. Only now did Donal bring forward his musketeers, ordering them to fire directly into the front line and the centre in particular. The advance began to falter, he gave the signal to charge again, and the real battle commenced. The men fought mostly hand-to-hand, while Donal and his senior colleagues engaged the English officers. They were Captain Malby, his brother the Earl of Conricarde, and some relations of William's, Burkes who had turned.

Outnumbered by at least five to one, Donal's men fought ferociously. He beheaded Malby himself, with one swing of his sword, while Burke set to work on his traitorous cousins, wounded two and killed one of them. Seeing their leaders fall, the troops lost heart and began to falter. Donal urged his men in for the kill then, and the enemy forces broke up and fled, leaving nearly four hundred dead and many more injured behind them on the field of battle.

After a headcount, Dermod established that the servants, women and horses were safe and that only fourteen fighting men had been lost. Many more, however, had been wounded. Donal ordered that they push on quickly, fearing that the English might regroup. All now bore the scars of battle in some form. Some of the men had lost too much blood and collapsed, and a few of the horses that had been hurt also went down, throwing their riders.

There was no alternative for these horsemen but to walk, laden down as they were with their armour. After a few miles tramping over the slushy ground, armour and any belongings were discarded.

The snow began to fall as night fell, the wind grew in strength and forced icy drops into their faces but there would be no stopping to make camp that night. More of the weaker men fell by the wayside, and by the time they reached Ballygar even Burke was pleading with Donal to stop for a while, but all entreaties were ignored. He seemed driven, and would not rest until they reached the northern slopes of Mount Mary, and the conditions had taken their toll on more of the group than anyone could accept. Dermod sought his nephew out to ask him what he was trying to do.

Donal looked a little disorientated. 'We have to keep moving, Uncle, that's all. Don't you know they are all around us?'

'But we are off track, Donal. We're heading west now.'

'No, we can't be. I've been following the marks.'

'It's impossible to see the marks in this weather. Now let's rest for a while, take stock and get our bearings.'

When they had eaten the scraps of food that were left, Donal and Dermod made a tour of the shrinking camp. The majority of the people were in a state of partial starvation and near total exhaustion. Some were sick, and all were mourning loved ones. As they left one group, Donal and Dermod turned to see Cait hobbling into the camp, supporting a Beara man with a leg injury. 'Cait' he exclaimed, 'What are you doing?'

'I couldn't leave Gearóid to die, could I? I've been helping him along for the past two miles.'

'I would have frozen without her help' Gearóid agreed bearing his teeth with pain.

'Well then stop that bleeding in his leg as fast as you can, and have something to eat. We will be on the move again soon.'

'No, Donal, we all need to rest.'

'Only for a short while. They'll be after us again come dawn, and I want to be away from this God-forsaken place.'

Returning to where William and Connor were resting, Donal and Dermod reported that there were only about one hundred and twenty fighting men left. 'I think' he said to Burke, 'That being so close to their homes, some of your men have left us.'

Burke's face darkened. 'Well I didn't see them go. It's more likely that they died, marching in these conditions.'

'Well we can't risk another encounter, anyway. They must know that we're heading for O'Rourke's country by now, and will expect us to take the most direct route. I would suggest that we head north, and then swing back to the east.'

'Are you mad? Didn't I tell you that there's nothing out there but bogs and lakes? If we got lost we wouldn't stand a chance.'

'We have to try, William, there is no alternative.'

They made their way through almost Arctic conditions. Snow came in squalls, blotting out everything, and vision was reduced to a few yards. The cold was severe, and even the hides that the marchers wrapped around their faces offered little protection; the first signs of frostbite began to appear, still some ate the snow through chattering teeth.

A lull in the weather sometime before noon brought the castle of the MacDavitts into view. They had gone over to the English side well before Kinsale, and Donal agreed when Burke commented 'We won't find any refuge at Glinsk castle. They would kill us before they would give us a morsel of food.'

'We'll have to try something, though' he said. 'Did we take the banners from Malby's men?'

'We did, and a couple of drums too.'

'Then we'll march up to the gates with them; they'll think we're English mercenaries seeking shelter.'

William was less than confident of the plan, but agreed to try it. The remaining force was organised behind Donal and himself, Dermod and O'Connor with flags flying and drums beating. The soldiers on the battlements seemed to accept their bluff, hailing them calmly, but then Colm MacDavitt appeared. 'Who are you, and where have you come from?'

Donal replied, having the best English. 'We are part of Captain Malby's force. We were following O'Sullivan and his men, but we lost them in the snow. Can you give us some food or shelter?'

MacDavitt turned to his companions and an animated discussion ensued. Then he shouted 'Come closer, the four of you.'

They hesitated for a moment before Donal grunted 'Move!'

As they approached the gate, MacDavitt asked 'Which section of Malby's force
do you belong to?'

'We are MacEgan's mercenaries.'

'I didn't know that MacEgan could afford mercenaries.'

'It must be some time since you were in contact with him.'

'Yes . . .' said MacDavitt doubtfully. 'Who is the man beside you?'

Burke blanched. 'Christ' he muttered. 'I tried to kill him once, years ago. I didn't think he would remember.'

Donal didn't pause, but answered 'He is Macleod, from Scotland. My right hand man.'

'To hell he is. He is William Burke, and he nearly killed me a couple of years ago.'

The alarm went up, and Donal and his followers turned and fled. Leaving the castle path they headed for the trees, but MacDavitt's men were close behind them, and filled with the spirit of vengeance.

Chapter Sixteen

Hunted

Charging through the woods, Donal could soon hear the shouts of those in pursuit and knew that they would be keen hunters. MacDavitt had an army of over three hundred at his immediate disposal, and was not only eager to settle old scores, and finish off the rebel force, but also to plunder the Spanish gold he knew them to be carrying.

Donal's men were forced to engage with MacDavitt's, and the escape attempt turned into a running battle conducted through woods and over marshes. It was hard going on the wet ground, and eventually the enemy force suspended their assault and withdrew to get some rest. Donal's party reached the higher slopes of Slieve Felim, and stopped there to try and sleep for a few hours. If they stayed where they were, they stood a good chance of remaining undetected as long as darkness remained.

A sudden change in the weather during the night brought torrential rain from the southwest, driven by gale force winds that were strong enough to uproot small trees. Soon, streams of water were running down the side of the mountain, and their little camp became waterlogged. Sleep was out of the question now, and all that they could do was try and keep the fires alight to warm themselves, and rest a little where they sat.

Shortly before daybreak the rain was tailing off, and the marchers were preparing to leave when a stranger suddenly appeared out of the trees. Donal looked up, alarmed. 'How did you find us?'

'It wasn't difficult. I saw you come in here last night. A bad night to be out in the open.'

'It was indeed' muttered Donal. 'What did you want?'

'I came to warn you that MacDavitt's men are less than a mile away. They intend to surround you here.'

'Are they that close?'

'They are, no doubt closer now. You need to move fast. I know these woods well, Donal Cam, and I can lead you out if you wish.'

Having built the fires up, so that it would look like the camp was still occupied, the small group quickly gathered and set off after Donal and his guide. Tramping through gullies and gorges, and over rushing streams, they finally emerged to the north of the wood (picking berries or anything to sustain them) from where they could see the soldiers approaching their camp. Praying to God that they hadn't been seen, they moved off at a fast pace.

MacDavitt, it seemed, refused to give up. Within a few hours he was on their trail once more, keen as a bloodhound. Donal stepped up the pace but still couldn't shake the army off. His own force was still dwindling, and the situation was growing more desperate by the hour. When the skirmishing began it took the form of vicious, hand-to-hand combat, and soon he had only about sixty fighting men left. Only when MacDavitt's force withdrew to count their losses and regroup did they manage to escape them, and throw them off their trail.

In the deep forest of Dubhbrack, they found refuge at last. Somebody managed to light a fire, but most simply collapsed and laid down where they were. The next thought was of food, but there was absolutely nothing left. After some thought, Donal ordered that the two the remaining horses be killed. More fires were lit and soon joints of meat were roasting and spitting over the hot flames. The smell half-sickened Donal, but he knew that there were no choices left. If they did not eat now they would be looking death in the face. Donal and Dermod sat down to their meal with heavy hearts.

'It tastes terrible' said Dermod.

'I know, and may God forgive us, but we have to eat.'

'There is hardly anyone left now, Donal.'

'I know. Cait tells me that the other two women died today; she is the only woman left.'

'My God. Will we ever make it to O'Rourke's country?'

'We have to make it now, Uncle. If we can keep MacDavitt off our backs it's only another day or two away.'

'And if we can't?'

Donal shook his head, and looked into the fire.

Early the following morning a few of the locals arrived carrying baskets of food. The plight of O'Sullivan and his followers was well known in the area, and they wanted to offer anything that they could spare. One of the men told them that MacDavitt's men had seen their fires. He had put them off, saying that the woodcutters from the village started the fires. Donal was overcome with gratitude, for as long as he sent some scouts out to observe the soldiers' movements they could rest there all day.

The scouts returned just before dark, with bad news. Captain Lambert, who had been billeted at Glinsk Castle, had dispatched search parties throughout the area. All the roads, bridges and fords were under guard. Donal sat with his head in his hands for a while, and then summoned his companions. He was further disturbed to see that, although Connor Kerry was still dressed in full armour, his feet were so badly ulcerated that he was having trouble walking. 'We have to evade Lambert's forces at all costs' he began.

Burke looked at him despairingly. 'How do we do that?'

'We move out now, as soon as it gets dark.'

'And what about Connor? He can hardly walk, and there are no horse left to carry him.'

'I can walk' Connor interjected. 'I'll have to, won't I, or lay down here to die.'

They set off in the half-light, but with the deepening darkness descended a thick fog and the marchers could hardly see the ground in front of their feet. They stumbled forward, probing the earth with long sticks, not knowing if they were following the right path at all. Just as the dreary sun began to drag itself over the horizon, a figure in a long white tunic rose up before them, materialising in the cold mist like some kind of spirit. Many of them blessed themselves, thinking that it was a messenger from God, or that they had already died, but then the figure moved closer.

It was an old man, who despite the climate was dressed in a loose, light garment and had nothing on his feet. A garland of rushes hung from his neck, and he was holding a staff. Donal finally gathered his wits enough to ask 'Who are you?'

The man gave him no answer, but replied 'I know that you are lost. I heard you passing my little shelter twice in the night.'

Realising that the man was one of the religious hermits he had heard about, who lived in the peace and solitude of the mountainside, Donal attempted to explain who they were. The hermit waved his hand dismissively. 'Let me show you the way' was all that he said.

They followed their guide in silence for a while, and then William Burke approached him. 'Do you know where we might find some food and shelter?'

'I am taking you to it' he replied. 'There is a small village over there in the valley, where you will be safe.'

The villagers, who were themselves dressed in little more than rags, gave them a warm welcome. Donal had never before encountered such squalor, but each of them was invited into someone's hut, where they squatted on the dirt floor and waited for oatmeal to cook on small turf fires. Some of them hung their clothes up to dry, but they knew they had only a few hours' respite.

When it was time to leave, several found themselves unable to rise. Connor Kerry admitted that he couldn't walk any further, and a litter had to be put together and four of the stronger men found to carry it. Before they departed, Donal pulled one of the older villagers to one side. Thanking him for all their generosity, he placed twelve gold coins in his hand, asking only that he showed them to no one until a week had passed.

They hadn't travelled far when the men carrying the litter began to complain of its weight. They were carrying not only the man in his armour, but also the belongings that he clutched to his chest. Donal looked at Connor. 'Is there nothing you can throw off, man, to lighten their load?'

He shook his head vehemently. 'How can I, Donal? 'Tis all I have in the world.'

Laughing, one of the men said 'Then when you die we'll have to bury you with your bags, and your armour on.'

Others laughed too then, and Donal wondered how long it had been since anyone here had done that. The humour helped them on their way.

About two hours later, they were covering some wastelands when they came across a blind, emaciated horse that had obviously been abandoned. He was nervous of their approach but didn't bolt, and finally allowed Donal to calm him with kind words and caresses. While he held the animal, Connor was lifted on to his back. He was mocking himself good-humouredly, a cripple on a blind horse, when Burke said 'Look over there; there's a man waving for us to come closer.'

'Be careful' Dermod warned as he reached instinctively for his sword, 'It might be a trap.'

'Let's get a little closer' said Donal, 'And find out for ourselves.'

Two well-armed scouts were sent forward, and having spoken to the man gestured for them to approach. The stranger greeted them, saying 'I know who you are, and I hear you're looking for O'Rourke's Castle.'

'We are' said Donal cautiously.

'I only wanted to tell you that it stands over there' he went on, pointing eastwards. Following his direction they saw the castle at last, rising up out of the mist like a mirage.

'Thanks be to God' said Donal with a sigh of relief, 'And thank you.' He handed the man a gold coin and they set off, their goal in sight.

Although the castle had seemed fairly near, the group were

walking like living corpses now and it took them over three hours to reach the gates. Everyone was concentrating simply on placing one foot in front of the other. Donal tried to calculate how long they had been walking. Could it really be the fourteenth of January?

As soon as they approached, some fifty people came out to help them but most refused to be aided, preferring to complete the journey on their own. It was a matter of pride, to have come so far at all. Of the one thousand and eighty who had left Glengarriff, only thirty-two men and one woman reached those gates.

Brian Óg O'Rourke embraced Donal, saying 'I thought you weren't going to make it.'

Donal gestured at his small group of followers. 'Not many of us did, my friend.'

'Is that a woman over there?'

'That's Cait. She has lost her husband and her two sons along the way but she's a fine, strong one.'

'She must be that. Now, come and fill your bellies, all of you.'

When they had eaten as much as they could, the travellers were offered hot tubs and clean clothes, and most of them made their way to their beds after that. Donal, however, felt refreshed and ready to talk over the situation with his hosts. As they sat by the huge fire drinking some good mead, Donal had his gold brought into the hall and showed it to the O'Rourke brothers there. 'With this' he said, 'We can build another army.'

Brian Óg was astounded. 'Have you not had enough of fighting, Donal?'

'No, Brian, the English won't quieten me until I'm in my grave.'

'Do you not think that the battle is lost?'

'To hell it is! O'Neill and O'Donnell may have given up, but I have not.'

'Well, then we'll help you in any way we can, but we don't have too much to offer. At the moment I can give you only thirty or so men, maybe ten horsemen.'

'That is a beginning, then. Thank you.'

Over the following days, while everyone recuperated at the castle, some of those who had disappeared came looking for refuge. Most were men who had deserted and headed for their homes, only to find their homes burnt down or their families gone. Some were the wounded, who had simply been unable to keep up with the group. Donal bore no grudges but welcomed them all equally. When he asked all of his followers if they would continue the fight against the English, however, less than thirty agreed. It was a bad blow, but Donal decided to bide his time. The suffering they had known was severe but suffering, he knew, is sometimes forgotten by a passionate heart.

Chapter Seventeen

Regeneration and Rejection

When Donal was told that Richard Tyrell was riding up to the castle, he felt that his prayers might have been heard at last. Tyrell was leading over two hundred horsemen, and two hundred galloglasses and servants. Although his defection had been a harsh blow at a bad time, Donal could not be displeased now that his captain had returned to him, and greeted him with warmth. 'It is a joy to see you here, my friend. You have come to join me again?'

'I have, Donal. I have a few loyal men here who fought with us in Beara, and some new recruits as well. They have all sworn to follow me to the gates of hell itself.'

'I am glad to hear that, Richard. Now, come and eat, and we'll make our plans.'

Over a lavish meal, it was agreed that Tyrell would go north immediately in search of Hugh O'Neill, who had, incidentally, been in debt to him since they were at Kinsale. While he was away Donal walked around the castle, giving each of the servants a gold coin, and visiting his own wounded men. Some had died and some recovered, and he decided to leave Cait to supervise the care of the rest. Then it was time to take stock of his new army, which had now been supplemented by five hundred fighting men who had fought with O'Neill and O'Donnell, and more than a hundred women and servants. A relatively small force, he knew it to be capable of defeating another of twice the size. Connor

Kerry's feet had healed and his uncle and William Burke had recovered from a mild fever. Brian Óg agreed that it was time to move out; together they would join Tyrell, and hope that O'Neill was waiting with him.

While preparations were underway, a shout went up that horsemen were arriving under the banners of the Maguires. The O'Rourkes were uneasy because Captain Lambert had been sighted about forty miles further west, but Brian Óg was soon reassured. 'That's Maguire alright' he smiled, 'I'd recognise the old devil anywhere.'

The large timber gates were opened and the motley army of two hundred or so crowded into the castle grounds, dressed in their own clothes and armed with a startling array of diverse weaponry. Hugh Maguire himself sat upright in his saddle like a knight in armour, his forehead balding and his long white hair and beard blowing in the wind. 'Welcome, Cousin' shouted Brian Óg.

'Greetings to you' he shouted back. 'And where is this O'Sullivan that I've heard so much about?'

Brian turned to Donal and laughed. 'He is not a man blessed with too much patience', he said.

When Donal went down to the bawn with his colleagues, Maguire had dismounted. Donal could not believe the size of the man, who was at least four inches taller than himself. He wondered why O'Neill, who was after all Maguire's father-in-law, had not brought him to Kinsale. Shaking him by the hand, the visitor said 'I'm glad to meet you, Donal Cam. I hear you accomplished great feats in arriving here at all.'

'My people showed great bravery' Donal replied simply.

'And where are you off to now?'

'To join up with Captain Tyrell, who went in search of O'Neill. He believes him to be in hiding somewhere north of Lough Neagh.'

'Ah, O'Neill has lost his fighting spirit, along with everything else. Tyrell is wasting his time.'

'I will find that out for myself, Hugh. Will you join us?'

'I will, but I may have to leave you once or twice along the way; I have a few scores to settle of my own.'

They headed north into unknown country, led by some local guides of O'Rourke's. The recent torrential rain had rendered the ground waterlogged and their progress was slow. With the rivers in flood, it soon emerged that their main route was cut off, and they were now in enemy territory; the Maguire Roes, close relations of Maguire and O'Rourke, had declared for the English. They had lately been joined by the O'Malachys and Lawrence Esmond, and could do some damage to Donal's force if their attack was unexpected.

Dermod was becoming anxious that the guides had lost their bearings in the wind and rain, but they insisted that they would soon be arriving at a river and eventually they did so. Some pontoons were commandeered, and the entire entourage negotiated the swollen river cautiously. As they regrouped on the opposite bank a scout came riding in with the news that the Maguire Roes and their allies were waiting for them at the ford further downriver. Brian Óg seemed unconcerned. 'Then they were waiting in the wrong place, weren't they. How many of them?'

'A strong enough force' the scout replied, 'A good few hundred including local kerns. Their main camp lies east by Cnoc Rua.'

'Well, we're only five miles or so from there. Will we pay them a visit, Donal?'

'I think we should, and let them know who's in control around here now.'

No sentries were on guard at the enemy camp, and it was an easy target. They killed or wounded about a hundred men without losing one, and took horses and supplies away with them as well as some booty. Hugh Maguire decided to take his men on further raiding expeditions to the north, while the rest of them headed east to make camp in the woods below Cuil Darach. During the night, the Maguire Roes managed to locate Donal's camp. He woke to the news that a powerful force was drawing up to their lines.

Sending two men to find Maguire and bring him back, Donal gave instructions to his people to mimic their earlier strategy, arming the women and servants with staves and lining them up behind the soldiers. Seeing what appeared to be a much larger force than expected, the Roes began to argue amongst themselves about the advisability of attacking; the bravery and ferocity of these men, after all, was well known.

The Maguire Roes seemed to be on the verge of an assault, when Hugh Maguire and his men came riding in from the north. Fearing that he was being surrounded by a superior force his cousin retreated, heading for Lough Erne to seek refuge in a small fort standing by the lakeside. The light was fading now, and instead of attacking at once Donal decided to leave them guessing for a while, and wait for a more opportune moment in the light of the following day.

The moment came the next morning, when the Maguire Roes began ferrying their troops to the islands. Donal attacked the fort with the combined forces, overcoming the enemy without difficulty. While Maguire stormed the islands with Dermod, his cousin somehow managed to escape in a boat with his two sons, but his army was soundly defeated.

Having avoided English troops movements, Donal and the others met up with Tyrell three days later. Hailing his friend, Donal's first question was 'Did you find O'Neill?'

'I did not, God damn him. I searched all over Slieve Gallon but there was no sign of him. I didn't even find the remains of a camp.'

'But he must have heard that we are looking for him?'

'I expected him to make contact somehow. We'll just have to keep searching.'

The continuous marching, in pursuit of the elusive O'Neill, was beginning to cause some discontent. Donal led the search for another four weeks before admitting that they were wasting their time. He couldn't believe that it was March, 1603 and so little progress had been made. Tyrell made one last journey out, while the rest of the force prepared to return to O'Rourke's Castle. When he had gone a scout came in with news of an English army, only three miles away and approaching fast.

Donal organised his men quickly, and when the troops arrived they were surprised to find them already prepared. They faltered very briefly, just as Donal gave the order to attack. After a perfunctory skirmish the English, seeing Tyrell and his horsemen riding in from the east, broke ranks and fled.

The news was bad; Donal could see it in Tyrell's face as they dismounted. 'Sit down' he said, 'And tell me.'

'O'Neill has surrendered to Mountjoy' said Tyrell bitterly. 'He went south to Mellifont some weeks ago, which is why we couldn't find him anywhere here.'

'Almighty God' Donal exclaimed, incredulously. He couldn't for the moment say anything more. Finally he looked up, asking 'Do you know what his conditions were?'

'The earldom of Tyrone has been fully restored to him' Tyrell replied, 'And he was granted lordship over Donal O'Cahan too. The Queen was evidently in a generous mood.'

'Then there is nothing we can do. Without O'Neill the fight is over.'

'It's true; we must sue for peace.'

An air of dejection pervaded the camp that night. The allies tried to make plans, but what was there to plan for? Some of them had lost everything, including their families and their homes. As they sat quietly around the fire, a rider came suddenly thundering in shouting 'The Queen is dead, Elizabeth is dead!'

Donal wouldn't believe the news until he had read the parchment that the messenger brought to him. Smiling, he confirmed that it was true. 'Elizabeth died two weeks ago. James Stuart is to be crowned at the end of the month.'

'I have visited James before' said Connor Kerry, 'I can go to him now if you wish it.'

'Right then, go and ask that out we be granted pardons, and our lands reinstated. Take some of this money, and dress yourself well before you appear before him. We will not be beggars before the Crown.'

The atmosphere in the camp was more hopeful, but it was still far from clear what might become of the allies. Over their meal that night Dermod asked his nephew what his plans might be.

'O'Neill is said to be on his way home' Donal replied. 'You and I should go and talk to him about our options. Burke and Tyrell, meanwhile, will ride to Dublin and sue for peace.'

'And the army?'

'It will have to break up. O'Rourke and Maguire can go their own ways and I'll pay the men off in the morning. We can't risk angering the new King, can we?'

'You're right' Dermod nodded, but there was despair in his voice.

His force dismissed, Donal retained twenty horsemen and fifty foot soldiers and servants and set off with his uncle to visit O'Neill. It was not a happy reunion. O'Neill felt shamed by the encounter, and made several efforts to justify his actions to his former ally. 'Don't forget, my friend' he said, 'I had my family to consider.'

Donal smiled sadly. 'My own family has scattered across the globe, Hugh. I have no idea how many of them are safe.'

'I know, I know, and I'm sorry. Now come and eat with me, and we'll talk of what our futures might bring.'

Donal sent for Cait, and with Dermod they stayed on with O'Neill for almost a month, until King James' court had been established. A letter from Connor Kerry told them that he had been well received, and that all his territories had been restored. The country seemed to be at peace, with only the O'Rourke's continuing the struggle now, and Dermod even felt confident enough to send for his wife and the rest of the family. Early in June, Donal and Dermod departed for London. When they arrived at the court, they were lavishly entertained while they waited for an audience with the King. On the fourth morning they were called before him.

The Irishmen felt out of place amongst the dignitaries, and were happy to see Connor coming to join them. 'I delayed my departure' he said when he had greeted them, 'So that I could present you to King James myself.'

'What is your opinion of him?'

'He's one of our own really, but the Queen's old favourites still hold all of the most powerful positions. He feels isolated, I believe.'

'So he has not yet imposed his will on the court?'

'No, not so far anyway.'

When their time finally arrived, Donal and Dermod were admitted to the great hall, and approached the throne with Connor at their side. Unsheathing their swords, they each went down on one knee and lay them, symbolically, before the King. They pledged their allegiance to him as they had been instructed to, and he welcomed them before examining a parchment handed to him by one of his attendants. When he eventually looked up at them there was a frown on his face. 'I am sorry to say that there is a problem here, gentlemen.'

Donal's heart sank. 'What is that, Your Majesty?'

'Your lands in Cork are now in the possession of Sir Owen O'Sullivan, a loyal subject whom I am told has served the Crown well. I am unable to simply evict him now. Your promise of obedience is duly noted, but I must reject your request. Instead, you will receive a pension of five hundred pounds per annum, for as long as you live, in return for your loyalty. Dermod O'Sullivan, you shall receive one hundred per annum.'

'Your Majesty...' Connor tried to intercede but James brushed him aside.

'That is my ruling' he said, 'Let my scribes record it thus.'

Donal was devastated, but managed to say 'Thank you, Your Majesty. I suppose that we can return to Ireland, if not to Cork?'

'That is correct' replied the King, 'And you are free also to travel without hindrance through any part of my kingdom. Good luck to you all.'

When they arrived at their lodgings, Donal and Dermod discussed their plight with Connor. With no lands of his own, and a pension that would hardly support him, Donal was inclined to head for Spain to join the rest of the family and their friends. Connor was ready, however, to try and convince the King to reverse his decision regarding their lands, and so they agreed to stay on for a few weeks in London.

With the passes that one of the King's aides had given them, Donal and Dermod were able to move at will through the streets of the town, to watch the ships coming in an out and even to access the naval dock. 'See what the Spaniards would have been facing' Dermod commented as they were watching the construction of a new warship.

'They're like floating batteries' Donal agreed. 'Twice the size of anything we have in Ireland.'

The following morning Donal and Dermod were summoned to the court for the second time. Connor had not seemed optimistic after his meeting with the King, and it seemed likely that they would merely be completing the formalities of their surrender. When they arrived the place was thronged with people, which was surprising considering the earliness of the hour, and Donal asked a passer by why the court was so crowded. It transpired that the King heard the complaints of his people on that particular day, and that they would have to wait in line along with everyone else. The minutes became hours, and when they were finally admitted it was only to be informed that King James had not changed his mind. They were shown into a small room where they signed pledges of allegiance and some documents regarding their pensions. 'We have been wasting our time here' said Donal angrily as soon as they were in the street. 'We'll leave for Ireland tomorrow.' He wondered, as they walked the streets back to their lodgings, if all his great plans had been nothing more than foolish dreams.

Chapter Eighteen

The Voyage

When King James learned of Donal and Dermod's imminent departure, he arranged for a royal escort to see them on to a ship that was sailing for the north of Ireland. His advisors were clearly asserting their own wills in this matter, but James felt that it was the least that he could do. He wished them well in their uncertain future lives.

O'Neill had not expected his guests to return, and was outraged that their lands had not been reinstated by the Catholic King. It was becoming apparent that the English attitude towards Ireland was not, in practice, going to change.

Over dinner that night, Hugh O'Neill turned to Donal. 'What do you plan to do now? You are welcome to stay here with me of course . . .'

'No, Hugh, though we are grateful for your hospitality. It seems that I can't return to Beara, as Owen is chieftain now, and my Spanish gold is fast disappearing. I have no option, I think, but to leave for Spain.'

'And your uncle, and the rest of your family?'

Donal looked at Dermod, who nodded. 'We will all be going together.'

Hugh looked at him thoughtfully for a moment. 'I am almost persuaded to come with you, my friend. I feel that my position here is not secure at all.' A surprised silence ensued, and O'Neill looked around the table until his eyes rested on the agitated face of his son, also named Hugh. 'Don't look so shocked, boy. You know as well as I do that they have already confiscated some of our best lands. The English have long memories and won't forget the trouble we've caused; there'll be no peace for us here.'

They talked long into the night, discussing their options. Red Hugh O'Donnell had died in Spain, and his younger brother Rory had been pardoned alongside O'Neill and granted the earldom of Tyrconnell. The last rebel against the Crown, Brian Óg O'Rourke, had defeated and killed Captain Bostock but then been betrayed by his half-brother, and finally died of a fever. There was no one left to lead the struggle now, and no question but that it was over. They would sail for Spain as soon as a suitable occasion materialised.

At the end of August a Spanish smuggling ship arrived at Lough Foyle. Word was passed around quickly that after offloading her cargo she would be returning straight to Spain. Donal immediately sent word to her captain, requesting that they be given passage, and soon had an answer. Captain Marquez promised to pick up any passengers in a small bay at the other side of Malin Head, where he would wait for two days.

All haste was made to pack what belongings the group had. They thanked Hugh O'Neill for his hospitality, and took their leave of him as he had decided to follow on at a later date. Supplied with a carriage, two guides and twenty horsemen, they set off towards Malin Head. They had to arrive by nightfall, and the horses were driven hard. Donal's main concern was that the carriage might lose a wheel or break an axle, and all of their possessions would have to be abandoned.

They pushed on relentlessly until they reached the shore at the appointed location, just as the darkness was beginning to descend. Seeing the ship at anchor Donal shouted in relief 'There she is, she's still there!'

'Light a torch, quickly' Dermod said to one of the men. It was held aloft and an answering light appeared aboard the boat.

'They've seen us' said Donal. 'Offload the carriage!'

A small boat arrived came in, empty but for two oarsmen. One of them waded up onto the beach, asking in Spanish 'How many?'

Donal looked round, and counting Dermod, his wife and two daughters, Cait and himself answered 'Six.'

'Very good' said the Spaniard, 'Only one trip.'

Loaded to the gunnels the punt left the shore, her oarsmen straining to move the weight. Luckily the water was flat calm. Donal asked them which port they came from.

'From Pontevedra' the sailor replied.

'We were hoping to get to La Coruña.'

'Don't worry, señor, we'll be passing La Coruña on our way to Pontevedra.'

When the boat scraped against the side of the ship, Donal was the first up the ladder and aboard, where the youthful captain greeted him. 'You were lucky, señor. I was about to lift anchor when I saw your light. My name is Captain Manuel Marquez, and this is my father's ship. He is ill at home, so I am making the trip for him.'

Donal looked at the man who stood no more than five foot six, and could only have been 27 or 28. He held out his hand, saying 'I am Donal Cam O'Sullivan, and I thank you for waiting.'

The captain shook his hand, and then said 'If you will excuse me, we must set sail. The cook, Luis, will look after you all until we are out of this inlet and have cleared the land.' Shouting orders to his crew, he strode away.

Luis showed Donal and Dermod to one small cabin, and the latter's wife and daughters to another that they would share with Cait. 'I'm sorry that they are so small' he said, 'The ship was not designed for passengers. Make yourselves as comfortable as you can, and I will bring you something to eat.'

'We are grateful, Luis' said Dermod.

In their little cabin Donal and his uncle felt like clumsy giants. Dermod shouted 'watch your head' as Donal was turning around but it was too late, and he laughed as his nephew rubbed his brow where he had walked into the crossbeam inside the door. 'You'll have to be more careful aboard.'

'I can see that. I'd better have the top bunk' he grunted.

'All right. I'm going to check on the family.'

The night was calm, almost too calm for the purposes of a smuggling ship. When Donal and his uncle came up on deck, the captain was cursing the lack of wind. Dermod tapped him on the shoulder. 'Do you want to bring us bad luck?'

'No, señor, but the sails are not even full.'

'Don't worry, there'll be a fine breeze out of the southeast before morning.'

'You have been at sea before?'

'Ah, I was a captain before you were even born' Dermod smiled.

As they reached the deeper water the wind increased slightly, and with the long Atlantic swell the Bonaventura took on a gentle rolling motion. As Donal returned to his cabin to get some rest, he came across Cait heading up on deck. She was very pale, and he took her arm. 'Are you alright?'

'No, I need some air. I think I'm going to be sick.'

'Will I stay up on deck with you?'

'No, no' was all that Cait managed to say as she retched, and ran for the ship's rail.

Dawn came, and as Dermod had predicted a strong breeze from the southeast was driving the sloop onwards at a steady six or seven knots. They were now about five miles off Aran Island, midway down the coast of Donegal and steering southwest towards Erris Head. Donal joined the captain, where he was yawning at the wheel. Stretching, he said 'We haven't discussed payment.'

'Your uncle and I agreed on two hundred and fifty reals.'

'That's fine. And did he ask you if we might call into Dursey on the way south?'

'He did. If we are to pick up more people they will have to

stay in the hold. Their payment can be discussed once they are aboard.'

The voyage along the west coast was uneventful, at least as far as they were aware. On the morning of the second day two sails were sighted about eight miles to the west, heading north. Donal could not have known, but it was Captain Cedro, sent from the Duke of Carazena with two ships carrying ammunition and thirty thousand pieces of gold. He had come to help Donal and Hugh O'Neill continue the fight. He was also unaware of the fact that, about two weeks previously, Cornelius O'Driscoll had arrived on Cape Clear Island on the West Cork coast. He was carrying guns and money that he'd collected in Spain himself. On hearing that O'Sullivan and O'Neill had sued for peace, he had gathered up his family, and about fifty young women who had been left widowed during the struggle, and set sail back to Spain.

On the morning of the third day the Skellig Rocks were sighted, and by nightfall the sloop had anchored in Kilcrovane Harbour, where they would be sheltered from the strong southerly wind. The locals, hoping that it might be loaded with contraband, launched a number of small boats from the village of Eyeries, not far from where the ruins of Dursey castle stood. Coming alongside, the first of them said 'Do you have something for us?'

'Nothing but ourselves' replied Donal, as he and Dermod leaned over the rail.

'It is ghosts I'm seeing' exclaimed the local man, turning to his companions, 'Or it's Dermod and Donal Dursey themselves!'

Their joy at seeing the O'Sullivans alive was tempered by the discovery that they were only stopping by on their way to Spain. While Dermod went ashore to seek out any remaining relatives who might want to go with them, Donal was making enquiries about his sister Síle and her husband, who had been taking care of his little boy. Soon afterwards he was riding east, having been directed to a small cabin on the shore near Ardea.

Donal rode for the rest of that late evening and night, taking directions three times. Finally, an hour or so before dawn he arrived at the hut, which was well hidden between two ridges of rock running down to the shore. Peering around in the dim light he could make out a little turf smoke rising from the hut, which was covered with green sods rather than thatch. By the tiny inlet a small boat was barely afloat on the coming tide. Dismounting, he whistled, waited, and then called quietly 'Síle, Síle are you there?'

After a moment a woman's voice asked 'Who's there? What brings you here at this ungodly hour?'

Donal smiled 'Don't you recognise my whistle, woman? Who do you think it is?'

'Oh God Almighty' the voice exclaimed, and a woman with a shawl flung over her nightdress ran out in bare feet and threw herself into her brother's arms.

When she stood back to look at her big brother, Donal enquired 'And where is your husband?'

Her face fell dramatically. 'Did you not hear? He died, two nights after you left. Slipped and fell from the cliff face when we were searching for food.'

'Oh, Síle, I didn't know. I'm so sorry for you. May God rest his soul.'

'Amen.' She blessed herself.

'And my son?'

'Ah, little Donal is a fine, strong boy now. He is sleeping soundly inside.'

Donal took a deep breath of relief. 'I will always be grateful to you, Síle. How did you manage?'

'I knew this place from my youth. The English are everywhere, but we are hidden here. With the money you left me I bought a little boat and I catch fish for us, enough to eat and sometimes to sell. We manage well enough. Now, come in and see your son.'

Within the hour Donal was on his way, with his son secured before and his sister behind him on the horse's back. Riding swiftly, they reached Eyeries soon after noon. When Dermod arrived he had several distant relations with him, and the beach soon became crowded with other local people who also wanted a passage to Spain. Taking his uncle aside, Donal hissed 'The captain has stipulated that he can take no more than a hundred in the holds. What are we going to do?'

'We'll just have to tell them the truth. Our own families must come first, and the others must argue it out amongst themselves.'

By the end of the day, after much discussion and a little violence, those that were coming aboard were being ferried out from the beach. There were now about one hundred and thirty passengers, but Donal was unable to force any one of them to stay behind, so determined were they to look for a better life elsewhere. Some carried nothing more than the clothes they wore, while others had food and cooking utensils as well as a change of clothing. Dermod had organised some men to fetch fresh food and water supplies, and the local passengers took leave of any loved ones.

When Donal arrived on deck, Captain Marquez was impatient to get under sail. He paid little attention to Donal's talk of extra passengers until he saw how much money was being offered to him. He raised his eyebrows, saying 'Thank you, señor; this is very generous. Let the people hurry aboard now, we must be well away by dawn.'

As the last of the passengers were picked up from the beach, some of those left behind made one last attempt to get aboard the Bonaventura, this time by pushing their way onto the punt. As the scene descended into chaos, Donal was forced to fire his musket in the air. 'Enough of this' he shouted. 'We are already carrying more than we should be. I will do my best to see that another ship comes for you soon, but now we must leave!'

Despite the cramped conditions, Cait had managed to settle all of the women and children into one of the holds by the time that Dursey was fading out of sight. There were so many men that they had to be divided into two groups, and would take turns sleeping in the other hold and up on deck. Donal and Dermod gave their own cabin up to family members, and slung hammocks up for themselves in the passageway.

For the first day they were blessed with fine weather, but most of the passengers still suffered some degree of seasickness. Donal spent his time with Síle and little Donal, getting to know his son. He sought Cait's company too, but she was very badly afflicted by the sickness and was mostly too weak to leave her bed.

The following afternoon the weather started to deteriorate, with the wind strengthening from the southwest. Soon the seas were swelling, and the ship began to rise and fall, burying her stem in the waves and sending spray breaking over the sides. Those who were forced to stay on deck had to take shelter, huddling together under the forecastle.

The winds abated overnight, and by morning only a medium swell was running. Remembering that his sister Orla had drowned one day out from Dursey, Donal asked that everyone say a prayer for her soul. One of the children had brought a bunch of wild flowers aboard with her, and as they prayed she cast them into the churning waters behind them. Donal gripped the rail tightly as he watched them drift, swirl, and vanish out of sight.

Chapter Nineteen

Exile

On the morning of the sixth day out of Dursey, the Spanish coast came into view. 'Cabo Ortegal' announced Captain Marquez with relief.

Donal looked at the horizon. 'How much further?'

'If the wind holds the same direction we should reach the approach to La Coruña by nightfall. We might be in the harbour by morning, but we'll have to wait there for official notice to go ashore.'

'My people are very anxious to be on dry land again, Manuel.'

'I know, there has been a lot of seasickness and we are lucky not to have lost anyone. We have to observe procedure, but I hope it won't take too long.'

When word spread that land had been sighted, many of the passengers came to the rail to see it for themselves. 'It looks like the Kerry coast' said one of them, 'Have we come back to Ireland?'

'It is Spain, you fool' laughed Donal. 'We'll be ashore soon.'

Some of the people were unsteady on their feet after being below for so long, others were sickened again by the intensified movement up on deck, and began to retch. Despite their weakness though, many were laughing now and clapping. It was good to see the land so near.

By early afternoon the wind had died down to a light breeze, and the ship wallowed sluggishly in the long swell. They were going nowhere, and everyone was disheartened by the realisation that their arrival would be delayed until at least the following day. The heat was oppressive, and the drinking water had been rationed.

At nightfall they were still about twenty miles from the harbour mouth. With no hope of making any progress in the darkness the captain ordered that the sails be lowered, and lanterns lit to alert other ships to their presence. Donal found himself unable to sleep and instead he walked the deck, wondering what lay ahead, what a life in exile might be like. After a while he was joined by Cait, who had brought little Donal up for some fresh air as he wouldn't sleep either. They sat down together, a strange kind of family, and watched the colours shifting in the foreign night sky.

The Bonaventura sailed into La Coruña at noon the following day. She signalled her arrival with two cannon shots, followed by another to indicate that there were passengers aboard. Dropping anchor about a mile from the shore, Captain Marquez explained that they would have to wait until an official came out to check the ship for infectious diseases. The land was so close, and it was a terrible frustration that they couldn't reach it.

The port official finally came alongside later that afternoon, and shuffled up the ladder with some difficulty. A heavy, swarthy man of fifty or so, it emerged that he was the captain's uncle. Embracing him heartily he said 'It's good to see you home safely, Manuel.' Looking around, he said 'Who are all of these people? You must have been mad to have taken so many passengers on board.'

'We were paid well' the captain replied, 'And they are important passengers. That man is Donal Cam O'Sullivan, Prince of Beara in Ireland, and an ally of the King's. The others are his family and friends, who were forced to leave their country because of English persecution.'

'My God, I must get ashore quickly and tell the Duke that we have such venerable visitors.'

Having greeted Donal and Dermod, the official climbed back into his boat and returned to the shore. After another three hours or so another boat arrived with fresh water and food supplies, and the charge hand took Marquez aside for a brief discussion. As he pulled away, there had still been no mention of their going ashore. Donal spoke to the captain himself, asking 'What was that about? What's happening?'

'I'm sorry, señor, but there is some delay. We have to wait until tomorrow morning, and that's all I have been told.'

'Jesus Christ, man, well can you arrange for a doctor to visit then? Some of these people need urgent attention.'

'The boat will be returning with more supplies soon. I'll send word to my uncle and he'll arrange something before too long.'

The doctor came out just before nightfall. He was a small, gruff man who was more interested in being on time for a dinner appointment than the plight of the sick passengers. Donal had to stress his own importance, and the fact that the doctor would be well paid, to see that they received adequate attention.

It was another night of frustration, eased somewhat by the provision of some wine and brandy, and a decent meal. Dermod felt apprehensive about what the problem might be, wondering if his people were somehow not welcome. When morning came and he saw the Bonaventura's own boats being lowered into the water, he went straight to Dermod's hammock and said 'There is something happening here that we don't know about.'

Rubbing his eyes, Dermod sat up slowly. 'What do you mean?'

'They are lowering the boats now, even though there has been no notification that everything is alright ashore.'

'Well it may be that there's something they can't tell us, but there's nothing we can do; we are guests here. We'll just have to wait and see what happens.'

As the day wore on and the powerful sun reached its peak, the patience of everyone on board was running out. Children were fretful and Cait was trying, unsuccessfully, to calm Donal's own son when he finally lost his temper. Striding over to the captain, he demanded 'What in the hell is going on, Manuel? Are we to wait for another day?'

Marquez smiled. 'No, Señor O'Sullivan, look towards the shore. The boats are on their way.'

Donal turned, and saw a flotilla of small boats approaching, bedecked with flags and bunting. 'What's going on, Manuel?'

'They are giving you a royal welcome, I believe.'

Donal stared in disbelief. 'My God . . . I must go and tell the others!'

'Yes, señor. And tell them that the Duke of Carazena has sent his own men to collect them.'

Donal and Dermod, who emerged from a cabin dressed like noblemen, were ushered aboard the Duke's own barge, and then the other passengers were transferred onto the remaining boats. As they approached the quay it became clear that an enormous party of welcome had been arranged, with the buildings decorated and the locals in their best clothes. As they stepped shakily ashore a great cheer went up. The entire entourage was led down streets lined with well wishers shouting 'Viva Irlanda', and throwing flowers. In the large square, two lines of soldiers were standing to attention, and about fifty yards ahead was a raised dais, where an elderly man sat in decorative robes. He was surrounded by attendants and an armed guard, and waved them forward as he struggled to his feet.

They bowed at the lower step, and the Duke welcomed them warmly. 'I am very sorry' he went on, 'That I was unable to send help when you needed it, but I could do nothing without the King's permission. When I finally sent Captain Cedro out, it seems he was too late to be of any use.'

'We understand, señor' said Donal, 'And are grateful for your recent effort. Can I ask, do you know where any of our children might be?'

'Most of them are in Salamanca, I believe, though not all. I sent a message to them yesterday, as soon as I heard that you had arrived. I think that your wife is there also. I'm sure you will meet them soon. How many of your people came with you?'

'About one hundred and thirty, señor.'

'Suitable accommodation will be found for them. Now, I would be happy if you and your immediate family members would accompany me back to the palace in my carriage. We would all be more comfortable out of this heat I think.'

The journey took about an hour, and while he made conversation about the voyage Donal was able to take in something of the countryside, which was showing the effects of a sustained heat wave. The earth was a rusty red, vines and olive trees were wilting and the cattle looked dehydrated and hungry. Men and women dressed in rough, dark clothing were hacking at the parched earth in a desperate attempt to prepare it for another crop. He was reminded of scenes from his youth, of farmers just as desperate but for different reasons, and of other, happier times.

When they were still at some distance from the palace, they could see the magnificent building looming up on a slope overlooking the River Breogan. 'My God' Dermod exclaimed, 'It's beautiful.'

'It is' Donal agreed. 'Far more beautiful than anything we saw in England.'

The Duke smiled. 'As you can see, we are nearing my palace. I have made arrangements for you and your families to stay here.'

'You are too generous' said Dermod, while Donal too expressed his gratitude.

'It is the least I can do. I will take my siesta now, and we will meet again at dinner.'

The O'Sullivans had never seen such a sumptuous, refined array of food as they did that evening. They ate many dishes that were new to them, and enjoyed a range of fine wines. Dermod was particularly happy to learn that his young son, Philip, had been sent to Salamanca to study, and was being well looked after by the Jesuits there. He was distressed, on the other hand, to hear that his daughter Leonora had entered a convent near Madrid. She was his favourite, and her letters to him had been full of her love for a Spanish nobleman, who was a first cousin of the King's. She had planned to marry him, and Dermod had of course approved.

The Duke was elderly now, and beginning to wander in his mind. He seemed genuinely delighted by the company of his guests, however, and assured them of every hospitable gesture. Their accommodation was more comfortable and luxurious than anything they had known before, and every effort was made to entertain them during their stay. After about a week, Donal got word that both Captain Martin Cedro and Cornelius O'Driscoll had returned from their abortive attempt to bring aid to Ireland. Requesting only two horses, Donal and his uncle rode the short distance to La Coruña to meet Cornelius. It was a strange new joy to ride out alone, without fear of attack.

'What the hell was I doing' laughed Cornelius, 'Rushing to bring you aid when you were sailing happily away in the opposite direction?'

'We hadn't heard that you were on your way, or we would have waited for you' Donal replied. 'As it was we had nothing left to stay for, and whatever King James might say we will never truly be forgiven by the Crown.'

'I know how it is, my friend. I have decided to make a life for myself here, too. What are your plans now?'

'We intend to move the family into new lodgings' Dermod interjected, 'And then seek an audience with King Philip, stopping to look for our children on the way.'

'Very good. I'll go with you if you wish, it's a long journey.'

'We don't mind that, Cornelius, as long as we are free men.'

Five days later, happy that everyone was settled into their new homes, Donal, Dermod and Cornelius set off in a carriage supplied by the Duke. Late that afternoon the weather broke at last. The skies darkened, and spasms of lightning heralded the onset of torrential rain. Soon the dirt road was a river, and rain was dripping into the carriage. Donal thrust his head out into the downpour and asked the escorting officer if there was a taverna nearby.

'There is one about seven miles on' he replied. 'We should reach it before nightfall.'

'Then send one of your men ahead, and tell them to expect us.'

They were glad to reach the shelter of the inn, where they changed out of their soaking clothes. They dined on young goat and chicken, with plenty of wine, and afterwards one of the local men took up his guitar. Some girls came round with the aguardiente, and soon everyone was singing or dancing. Even Donal contributed some old Irish songs.

Having been unaware of the strength of the local firewater, he woke in the morning with a dry mouth and a pounding head. Swinging his feet out of the little bunk he tried to stand up, almost lost his balance and sat down again cursing. 'Jesus Christ, my bloody head.'

'I'm feeling the same' croaked Cornelius. 'I don't remember coming up here last night, do you? We'd better ask for some of that coffee. They say it is the best cure.'

'If Cait were here she would cure me with her herbs, and I'd be fine in an hour or two.'

'Well, she's not here' said Dermod, 'So you'll just have to suffer. Come on, we must eat something, and then be on our way.'

The jolting of the carriage as it bounced and scraped over the rough road added to their discomfort, and in the end Donal decided to change places with one of the escort riders. The wind would clear his head faster, he thought, and in a way he was more comfortable on horseback anyway.

Later that day, the pealing of church bells indicated that they weren't too far away from their first destination. Soon, the city of Santiago de Compostela came into view, and then they were moving through the narrow streets towards the eleventh century cathedral. 'I suppose that we should go and thank God that we are still alive', said Dermod. Brushing the dirt from their clothes, they got out of the carriage and headed in the same direction as the crowd of pilgrims in the square.

They were on the steps when they heard someone shouting in Irish, 'Father, is that you?'

Turning sharply, Dermod exclaimed 'My God, it's Fineen and Seamus!' He opened his arms to his sons, who embraced him and their cousin in turn. They entered the cathedral together, to offer sincere gratitude for their meeting, and then adjourned to a taverna, where they could eat and exchange their news.

They spent the rest of the evening together, talking avidly. Dermod told them about their hazardous march and gave them news of their mother and sisters. Donal related the story of the fall of Dunboy which led Fineen, shyly, to enquire after his cousin's deformed twin. Donal was quiet for a moment before answering. 'He wouldn't leave the castle, Fineen, wouldn't even leave his room. When the castle went up, he went up with it.'

Dermod broke the uneasy silence that followed. 'So tell me, boys, why has your sister decided to become a nun? Did he leave her at the altar steps, or what?'

'No, Father. He was a hot-blooded man, and he was killed in a duel about three months ago. Leonora was broken hearted, and she only wants to lock herself away from the world.'

'I'm sorry to hear that. You must go and tell your mother and your sisters all about it tomorrow, while we go on to Salamanca. For now, we must all get some sleep.'

In his bed that night, Donal reflected on finding himself in this foreign country. What did the future hold? Why had his sons not come to meet him, and would they ever make a life for themselves in this hot, fast, colourful place? It was a long, hard path he had trodden to get here, and along the way he had lost more loved ones than he could bear to number. Could this strange land be where he would come, finally, to rest?

Chapter Twenty

Spain

The journey to Salamanca took nearly five days, the continuous rain having left the roads in a very poor condition. They had stopped at Orense and Zamora on the way. Gazing from the carriage window at the walled city of Salamanca, high on its perch over the plain below, Donal was amazed. 'The Spanish really take advantage of the natural outline of the land, don't they?'

Cornelius O'Driscoll nodded. 'They are master builders, certainly.'

Having crossed the river, they began the steep climb to the city. They arrived at the main doors of the Collegio de los Irlandeses during siesta time, and no one responded when their officer rang the bell. Donal climbed out himself, taking his sword and banging the door with its handle. Eventually a small grille was pulled back, and two eyes appeared. 'What do you want? If you are looking for accommodation, there is none.'

'I am Donal O'Sullivan, Prince of Beara, on my way to visit the King. This is my uncle, Dermod, and he wishes to see his son.'

'Oh Mother of God help me' muttered the voice, and a commotion behind the doors heralded their opening. A portly priest waddled out as fast as he could, blessing the visitors and talking rapidly. 'My dear friends in God, forgive me I beg you, we are accustomed to taking our rest at this time of day and I was not properly awake when you called. Welcome, welcome all of you to our humble dwelling, I would be honoured if you would grace us with your presence this day . . .'

Into the middle of this outpouring rushed a boy shouting 'Father, Father', and Dermod found himself with his son in his arms.

'Philip, my boy, I am so glad to see you. How do you like it here?'

'I like it well enough' Philip replied, 'But I have missed Beara, and the family. Where are the rest of them?'

'We are all in Spain now, and intend to stay.'

In the refectory, the visitors were introduced to students from all over Ireland, many of them from West Cork. They were shown to their rooms, where they rested and changed, and then seated at the high table for dinner. Donal was anxious to push on to Madrid, but agreed to stay on for a few days so that Dermod could spend some time with his youngest son.

While they were there, Donal took the opportunity to learn all that he could about the current situation in the country and at the Royal Court. Father Paulo, whose brother occupied the position of confessor to the King, was particularly informative. Philip, he said, was a pious and charitable man, but an inadequate monarch. He had squandered funds, and done nothing to ease the country's financial problems. Aware of his shortcomings, he had passed most of his responsibilities over to his Court favourite the Marquis of Denia, Francisco Gomez de Sandoval y Rojas. Unfortunately the Marquis, too, was unsuitable. Donal listened intently to everything he was told.

The journey to Madrid was another long and torturous one across a high plateau of land. Having reached Avila after two days, they decided to stop there and rest for a day. Dermod stayed at the taverna, while Donal and Cornelius decided to visit the shrine of St Teresa, and ask for her blessing on all those left behind in Ireland.

Three days later they arrived at the gates of the Escorial palace.

It loomed above them with its three towers, at the peak of a mountainous slope. Having reached their destination at last, they were summarily turned away. The King, it seemed, was unwell and not seeing visitors until the following week. They had no alternative but to go on to Madrid, and wait to be summoned.

Madrid was a city in the process of reconstruction. There was a great deal of activity and of dust, and it took them some time to find their lodgings. Water was a precious commodity after the long, hot summer, and at first they couldn't even wash themselves properly. Not knowing when they might be called, they were unable to roam far from their given address. Finally, word arrived that they were to present themselves the following morning. With a journey of over four hours to consider, they decided to leave soon after midnight to ensure an early audience.

The palace shimmered in the early morning mist. Being expected, they were quickly admitted and led through a long corridor to the basilica. Padre Juan introduced himself to Donal, Dermod and Cornelius, who were all in awe of the grandeur surrounding them. 'I have arranged for you to see the King in about half an hour' said the Padre, staring at Donal. 'If you don't mind me saying so, senor, you bear a remarkable resemblance to the monarch.'

Donal smiled. 'I do?'

'Yes, quite remarkable. You are a little taller, but . . .'

Due to some alterations that were taking place, King Philip received them in the main library, which was already full of people. They were announced, and as they walked the length of the hall the people turned to stare. When he saw the King, Donal could quite understand why. The build, the facial structure, even the beard; It was like looking in a mirror.

Philip greeted his visitors cordially, though he too had obviously been struck by his resemblance to Donal. Composing himself, he said 'I welcome you all, my Irish friends.'

'We thank Your Majesty for receiving us' said Donal with a bow.

'I regret that I was misinformed about the situation in Ireland, and could not have offered you more assistance.'

'We are aware that you were misled, Your Majesty.'

'You can be assured that the culprit, Don Juan de Aquila, has been punished. I know now that you fought valiantly on my behalf, and as a sign of my gratitude I intend to knight you, and further to award you the Cross of Santiago for your efforts. Both you and your uncle will receive a handsome pension.'

Donal was speechless. Padre Juan indicated that he should kneel and he did so, blindly. The short ceremony was complete, and he was walking out through the library doors again before he really knew what had happened.

Donal returned to Salamanca a Spanish Knight. It was time to decide what their long term plans might be, and there were so many of his fellow countryfolk living in the walled city that he and Dermod felt quite at home there. With the assistance of the Jesuits they found suitable accommodation for the family on the Calle Veracruz, and then Donal set off in search of his sons.

When he arrived at the old Court in Valladolid, which was now occupied by the Duke of Carazena, Donal understood why young Dermod, Donnell and Teige had failed to come looking for their father. They were leading full and exciting lives there, and busy raising funds for Ireland. Donal forgave them, and in addition he forged a friendship with the amiable Duke that was to last for years.

Recognising that he could not persuade his sons to leave Valladolid, he stayed on with them for as long as he felt able. Over the next few years he divided his time between the old Court and his family home in Salamanca, and paying occasional visits to the King and the friends he had made in other cities. His greatest sadness was that his wife flatly refused to accept his son, Donal, into the family. It had fallen to Cait, who had herself remarried by now, to raise the boy as her own. His children were each getting married in quick succession, and he was particularly proud of the match that his daughter Juliana had achieved. She was married to the Duke of Córdoba, who was in residence at the Alcazar de los Reyes, and Donal spent an increasing amount of time living with the couple there.

It was while he was staying at Córdoba once that his eldest son, Dermod, came to visit him. He had married the daughter of the Duke of Melina de Sedonia, and Donal knew it to be a happy match but could see that there was something wrong. After some coaxing, and a dose of strong wine, Dermod explained that his daughter, Isabella, was in trouble. 'You know how headstrong she is, Father, you know what she's like.'

'I do. What has she done now?'

'Well ... It seems that she slept with my wife's brother, Ricardo, when he was staying with us six months ago, and now she finds herself pregnant.'

'My God, Dermod, what possessed them?'

'I don't understand it either. He is far older than she is, and has only been widowed a year. Now she says she wants to marry him. What can I do?'

'You must prevent it at all costs. The blood is too close.'

'I have tried talking to her, and so has her mother. She pays us no heed. She admires you though, Father. She might listen to you.'

Donal thought for a moment before replying. 'I'll come back with you, Dermod, but I don't know that I can help.'

His journey was in vain. Isabella locked herself into her room and was refusing to talk to anyone. Only a servant was allowed in to bring her meals, and a week into Donal's visit she announced that she would kill herself if she were not allowed to marry Ricardo.

Donal couldn't bring himself to stay for the ceremony, which was to be held in the private chapel a few days later. He left his son's house sadly, to attend to some business in Madrid, and then went on to the Monasterio de Santa Maria de El Paular. Close to the riverbank there, amongst the vines and olive trees, he had built a new home for his wife. When she was settled he took off for the Court once more; the couple had not been intimate for many years now, although they remained fond of one another and Donal took every care to ensure Ellen's happiness.

On his trip to the Court he experienced something of the bitter rivalry between those who sought to exert their influence upon the King. The Duke of Lerma, who would in turn be passed over in favour of a friend of Donal's named Zuniga, ousted Francisco Gomez. Spain's power was in decline, and the coffers were emptying fast. The Court could no longer afford to provide such lavish hospitality, and Donal decided to move on. His youngest son Donal had now followed his cousin Philip to the Irish College in Salamanca, and he would visit him there.

Donal and his son were walking in the gardens a few days later, when a messenger arrived with the news that his wife had died suddenly. Having sent word to the rest of the family, they returned immediately to the new family home to make funeral arrangements. Ellen, her maidservant told him, had been out walking alone on the previous afternoon. When she failed to return two men went out after her, but by the time they found her body it was cold.

Donal sat by the coffin for a long time, watching the shadows gather over his wife's face. It had not been a passionate union, not since he'd met his other, beloved Ellen anyway, and she had been forced to forgive him many infidelities. But they had loved one another in their way. He kissed her frozen forehead, and then allowed the coffin to be removed to the nearby monastery.

It was a small party that gathered for Ellen's internment in a hastily constructed vault in the monastery grounds. Of all the children they had together only Juliana attended, and Donal was both hurt and ashamed. Immediately after the funeral he changed his will, removing Donnell and Teige from it altogether.

Some six months later a message came from the Court stating that King Philip wished to see him there. This had never happened before, and Donal began to wonder if the English King might, at long last, have changed his mind about the lands in

Cork. Philip soon dispelled his hopes, however. Receiving him in his own rooms, he indicated a seat. 'I wrote to King James on your behalf once again, Donal.'

'That was very good of you' he replied. 'Has he answered you?'

'He has answered in his own hand, and told me that he would, himself, be happy to reinstate your lands. The opposition of his advisers, however, remains too strong. His hands are tied, Donal. I think you must accept this as his final decision, my friend, I'm sorry. I have decided to make you Count of Berehaven myself, at a short ceremony to be conducted in the near future. I hope this will ease your disappointment.'

As he made his way home, Donal realised that Philip was right. All hope of returning to Ireland was gone, and he must accept that like his wife he would die on Spanish soil. His whole family had made lives for themselves there, after all, and he had many relations and friends all over the country. He had to admit, furthermore, that he was getting old and tired, and that it was time to sit back, and rest, and enjoy all that he had earned.

Over the next months Donal spent more and more time at the monastery, and became so devout that he was accustomed to attending three or more masses each day. He knew himself well enough to recognise that some of his past actions still weighed on his conscience, and that he was making his peace with God. He also began to pledge substantial portions of his wealth to the poor. When his sons heard this, unaware as they were of the changes to his will, they travelled to the house to confront him.

Donal had not forgiven his sons, and was further angered by this display of selfish greed. He removed himself to the monastery, and refused to see them at all. While they were together after so long apart, the young men decided to stay at the house for a few days and celebrate their reunion. Donal's young cousin Philip arrived from Salamanca to join them.

In the course of the celebrations, a serious argument arose between Philip and a member of the household named John Bath, who was a descendant of the MacGillicuddy O'Sullivans of Desmond. A large amount of wine had been consumed, and the two men began to argue about Donal's title as Count of Berehaven. Hearing that violence had erupted, Donal hurried back to his estate. There he found Philip and John with swords drawn, and his anger boiled over into rage. 'There will be no blood spilt in this house' he roared. 'All of you can leave now, and that includes you, John!' Struggling to come between the two protagonists, he turned towards his son Dermod to appeal for his help, but John Bath would not be calmed. Dropping his sword, he pulled out a dagger and launched a frenzied attack on his patron, stabbing him repeatedly in the neck and back. Dermod was beside him in a second, and managed to knock the dagger from his hand with his own sword, but Donal was already slumped on the floor with blood flooding out around him.

The young men gathered around the older one, silent in their horror. John Bath ran from the room, and for now they let him go. Philip began to weep, and then to repeat 'What have I done? What have I done?'

Donal felt the life seeping out of him, and recited Our Father in Latin, his voice fading with his will to live. Many, many times he had stood on the edge of death, and now it was time to let himself fall. He saw visions of the family and friends who had gone before him, saw his beloved Ellen waiting for him with open arms. Raising his own, as if in greeting, he slipped away.

A requiem mass was conducted a week later, at Salamanca, by Archbishop Mendoza himself, and was attended by all of Donal's relations, friends and allies in Spain. The King was represented by Zuniga, and decreed that Donal should receive full military honours. Privately, Dermod, vowed that he would go after John Bath, find him and avenge his father's death.

When the family gathered afterwards at the Irish College, to hear Donal's will, they were shocked by its revelations. Although his eldest son Dermod was to receive his titles, Donal had left the entirety of his wealth to the College, to further facilitate the education of Irish exiles. Even the family home had been willed to the College, and there would no longer be any focal point for gatherings. By their earlier omission, his sons had effectively split the family apart, and they parted on far from amicable terms.

Donal's eldest son, nevertheless, was true to his word. He sent spies out all over the country, and whenever he received any reports of John Bath's movements he pursued them diligently. It was on the foot of one such dubious sighting that he found himself in a taverna, in the Latin quarter of Madrid, one hot summer night. Coming across some drunken brawl by accident he was stabbed in the heart, and died almost instantaneously.

With Dermod's death, young Donal inherited his father's titles even though he was illegitimate. Donnell and Teige disappeared from the annals, when they went to serve Spain in her foreign wars. Philip stayed in Salamanca, and tried to maintain some contact with Donal, who would visit his adoptive mother Cait at her home near La Coruña, but then seems also to have vanished. The large and powerful clan of Donal Cam O'Sullivan, Prince of Beara, was scattered at last as dust on the cold winds of Irish history.

BANTRY BAY

Twixt Kilcrohane's bleak headland bold
and Beara's wilder shore
where stately hills majestic rise
whose tall peaks skyward soar
whose heights among the curlews green
Or hoarser eagles call
In concert wild do reverberate
o'er rock nod waterfall.
In beauty ope's the wild expanse
of Bantry's noble Bay
where rippling waves and billows bright
Round verdant islets play
across its bosom rolling wild
fair blows its balmy gate
that wafts its azure waters bright
o'er the fishers fragile sail
and gaily o'er its fleecy surge
The seagulls wings in flight
or gently glide through foam and spray
with furled plumage bright
Full many a bright and glorious spot
of beauty and romance
lies strewn on the rugged border
of that broad bays expanse
and all around its margin fair
stands many a ruined hoary
of stately piles of former days
of fame pride and glory.
Each hallowed by some legend old
or tales of ancient days
when proudly o'er his wild domain
famed Beara's chief held sway

that far extent of scenic strand
that breasts the water heaves
from Bantry's old historic quay
to Beara's deep ocean caves
By fair Glengariff's sylvan slopes
its silvery surges roar
while calm and stilly sleep
its waves by lonely Adrigole
its glistening billows softly heave
by lonely dark Dunboy
where nobly perished Donal Cam's
brave band of cavalry
and by Muintir Mhaires rocky point
where the ocean breakers bound
and the wild Atlantic's murmurings
unseethingly resound
white gleams the foam upon the beach
along the Southern strand
laved by the softly swelling tide
of waters smiling bland
and inward to that quiet spot
The Abbey Churchyard lone
where through the stately elm trees
The night winds sadly moan
among records of the olden times
of fame renowned and glory
Enshrined the name of Bantry Bay
in history's secret story.
For its circling hosts of guardian hills
oft in days of yore
re-echoed to the sound of strife
and heard war's thunder roar
when kingly chief and clansmen bold
for to guard her cragbound coast
with native valour battled there

against fierce invading hosts
and they long centuries ago
Did see St. Patrick sail
To freedom, ere his coming
brought faiths light to the gael
And the doleful sight in scattered bands
saw the wild geese fly
far away from their native homes
To a foreign land on a
battle field to die
Still Bantry Bay's blue waters
are rolled brightly as they roll
When deeds of fame and chivalry
were rife in days of old
And brightly still the summers sun
illumines the landscape round
where the relics of a mighty past
strew all that storied ground
And chiefs of might and warrior men
Have all passed away
And tranquil peace prevails
both wave and brotherland today